"Here's your problem."

John waved his hand toward the engine. "No fan belt."

"Can you fix it?" Victoria asked tightly, her eyes focusing on his full and sensual mouth.

"Yeah. I'll have to rig up something . . . say, two inches wide." His eyes narrowed as they skimmed down her torso. "Then again . . ." He reached out and clasped her waist.

Victoria stiffened at the warmth of his hands.

"Hey, whoa, there." John squeezed a little. "I'm not going to hurt you. I just wanted to measure—" The words stuck in his throat. What he just wanted to do was exactly what he was doing. Touch her. . . . He yanked his hands away. "Never mind. It's too small, anyway."

"What?" Victoria's voice was hardly more than a whisper.

"Your belt." He grunted. "Your waist isn't any bigger than a skinny twelve-year-old's."

As John stomped off to his truck, Victoria looked down. Surely his hands had left burn marks. . . .

Candace Schuler began writing romance novels about eight years ago, with the encouragement of her husband, Joe. An accomplished and very popular Temptation writer, she creates stories that have both humor, great emotional intensity and vivid sensuality. Candace and Joe travel widely and have lived in many parts of the U.S. Recently they settled near San Francisco, and Candace is particularly pleased to be back in her home state.

Books by Candace Schuler

HARLEQUIN TEMPTATION
28–DESIRE'S CHILD
102–DESIGNING WOMAN
129–FOR THE LOVE OF MIKE
183–HOME FIRES

Soul Mates

CANDACE SCHULER

Harlequin Books

TORONTO • NEW YORK • LONDON
AMSTERDAM • PARIS • SYDNEY • HAMBURG
STOCKHOLM • ATHENS • TOKYO • MILAN

To Joe,
husband, best friend, cheerleader,
slave driver, soul mate

Published June 1988

ISBN 0-373-25305-2

1

VICTORIA DILLON STOOD bareheaded under the scorching Arizona sun, silently debating the fate of her last remaining bottle of Perrier. Should she use it to quench her own thirst, or would it do more good in the radiator of her overheated Mercedes?

She'd already depleted the gallon jug of water brought along for just such a purpose about twenty miles back. The melted ice from her small cooler had been sacrificed five miles ago. All to no avail. The temperature gauge on the dashboard had barely had a chance to register normal before it began climbing back into the danger zone.

She'd pulled over to the side of the road for the third time, trying not to let the billows of steam rising from under the hood of the sleek white car throw her into a dither. Dithering would get her nowhere, she told herself sternly. But what Victoria Dillon knew about cars could have fitted, with plenty of room to spare, into the cap of the Perrier bottle she was holding.

It was damnably hard not to dither.

She lifted her free hand to shade her eyes and peered down the road in both directions for the fourth time in as many minutes. Nothing. No buildings, no cars, no discernible life forms of any kind. Just a two-lane blacktop highway that stretched into infinity in either direction, and a barren red-dust desert that went even farther.

The last car she had seen had passed her thirty minutes ago at best. The last human beings she had seen had been two small Indian boys tending a flock of dusty sheep, and that had been before the car passed her. Way before. She could, she realized, be stranded for hours before anyone came by to help her. Supposing anyone would even stop to help her when they did come by.

"So, okay," Victoria said to the open hood of the car, "let's consider our options."

There weren't many.

She was stranded in the Arizona desert under a blazing June sun, smack dab in the middle of the Navajo reservation, with no water, no knowledge of the high-powered car she drove, except where to put the gas in it, and not a mechanic or service station in sight. What she did have, however, was one six-ounce bottle of orange-flavored Perrier, slightly less than a quart of warm Diet Coke and an owner's manual for the Mercedes. Somewhere.

Victoria sighed loudly, allowing herself a tiny moment of self-pity, and then straightened her shoulders.

"Glove compartment," she mumbled, deciding on the most likely place to look first.

She reached under the gaping hood, setting the bottle of Perrier on the flat surface of the air filter, and went around to the passenger side of the car. Yanking open the door, she plunked herself on the red leather seat. It was hot, warming her legs uncomfortably even through the fabric of her crinkly cotton skirt. Hurriedly she popped open the glove compartment and rummaged inside for the owner's manual.

Surely it would give her a clue as to what was wrong with her mechanical steed, she thought, flipping through an untidy pile of folded maps, motel brochures and gas receipts as she searched for it. All she had to do was read it and—voilà—problem solved. Or at least problem defined, which was a step in the right direction.

When she finally found it, the manual listed several possible causes for the engine to overheat, aside from the most obvious one of there being no water in the radiator. But she already knew that wasn't the problem.

A leak in the hose was listed as a possible problem. But how could you tell if the hose had a leak? She bent over, sticking her face as close as she dared to what she assumed was the radiator hose. It looked fine to her. Fat, smooth and black, presumably connected at both ends to whatever it was supposed to be connected to. With the tips of her thumb and forefinger she jiggled it gingerly, just to be sure. Yes, it was definitely connected. She squeezed it lightly, testing for leaks. Nothing happened.

So far, so good.

She straightened, absently lifting the heavy sheaf of midnight hair off the back of her neck with one elegant hand as she read down the text to the next item.

"Check the fan belt," it said. Victoria squinted under the open hood of the car again, wishing she had paid more attention the few times anyone had ever discussed the finer points of car repair in her presence. A little knowledge would have come in handy about now.

She let her hair drop back into place and leaned farther over, lifting her sunglasses out of the way as she peered at the engine.

Where the hell was the fan belt? What did it look like? And what was she checking it for, anyway?

She shuffled around the left fender, her body bent sharply at the waist to keep her clothes from brushing against the car, and stuck her head farther under the open hood. So engrossed was she in her effort to locate the fan belt that she failed to hear the soft crunch of tires as a truck pulled off the road behind her.

AT FIRST IT WAS JUST a white dot on the side of the road, an indistinct blur on the far horizon, wavering like a mirage in the intense summer sun. As he got closer he thought it might be a lone horse or, perhaps, a sheep that had wandered away from one of the flocks that grazed the reservation. He slowed down in case the animal suddenly took a notion to dart onto the road. But it grew larger and more distinct as he drew nearer, arranging itself into the sleek lines of a white 450 SL hardtop convertible. Very nice, he thought, taking in the shiny gold pinstriping and the discreet Mercedes insignia that decorated the trunk. A little flashy, maybe, but nice.

Nice, too, was the rounded female fanny sticking out into the road. It was draped in a white skirt made of some gauzy material that, because of the wearer's bent-over position, dipped nearly to the ground in front while leaving a sleek pair of legs bare to above the knees in back.

They were good-looking legs, he decided as he slowed his truck. Gorgeous legs, actually—long, tanned and lean. The gentle swell of the calves were set off by the braided ankle ties of a pair of flat white sandals. His lips pursed in a silent whistle of appreciation. In a pair of high heels those legs would bring traffic to a dead stop. They were bringing him to a stop without the heels. But then, John Redcloud had been a leg man since puberty.

He pulled up behind the disabled Mercedes, wondering if the rest of the woman would live up to the promise of those gorgeous legs. Wondering, too, what she was doing out here all by herself.

The desert wasn't a place for people to be on their own, especially if they didn't know how to take care of themselves. And one look at the car and the woman— what he could see of her—told him that she didn't. The gauzy white summer skirt, the flimsy sandals, the flashy gold-trimmed car told him all he needed to know. *City woman.* Out here by her lonesome, she was as helpless as a newborn lamb. Except that even a newborn lamb had enough sense to stay with the flock.

Grabbing the straw cowboy hat off the seat beside him, John shouldered open the door of his dusty Chevy pickup. His booted feet hit sunbaked earth with the soft thud of a cat jumping from table to floor.

Fully engrossed in whatever she was doing under the hood, the woman didn't look up.

If I were a snake . . . John shook his head, not finishing the thought. He jammed on his hat, pulling it well down to shade his eyes from the blazing sun, and slammed the door of his truck.

The woman jumped and jerked upright, barely missing whacking her head on the open hood as she turned toward the unexpected sound.

The promise of her legs had not been an empty one.

She was reed slender, as elegant and as delicately built as a Thoroughbred mare. The gauzy material of her skirt swirled at her sudden movement, billowing out before it settled around her legs. Its matching boat-necked top was neatly tucked into a wide yellow belt that wrapped twice around an impossibly narrow waist.

Her shiny hair, raven black and almost Indian straight, fell from a precise center part to brush against her shoulders. The classic pageboy style and feathery bangs framed the sharp elegant bones of her face, giving her the look of an ancient Egyptian priestess. From where he stood, John could see that her lips were red and glossy, her skin smooth and lightly tanned, her high cheekbones delicately flushed from the heat.

She held a small open book in one hand. The other was upraised, her slender arm crooked at the elbow, thumb and forefinger holding a pair of ridiculously oversize sunglasses against her forehead.

She looked, he thought, exactly like an ad for an expensive perfume in one of those trendy fashion magazines, as if she had been deliberately posed against the harsh desert landscape to emphasize her delicacy and elegance.

John sighed heavily. He had a weakness for elegant women with delicate builds. Especially ones with gorgeous legs. With the slightest bit of encouragement from the owner of a pair of legs like that, he could be tempted to forget a lot of hard-learned lessons about city women...about Anglo women. Hell, about women in general. It was undoubtedly a damned good thing that this was destined to be a brief encounter, he told himself sternly; otherwise, he'd be tempted to get into all kinds of trouble. Again. With another heartfelt sigh, John adjusted his hat more firmly on his head and started toward her.

At his first step Victoria dropped her sunglasses into place on the bridge of her nose and tented her hand above them in an effort to see past the glare of the sun.

The man walking toward her was very tall, his height exaggerated by the curved heels of his cowboy boots and the battered straw hat on his head. He wore faded dusty jeans, the kind that molded themselves to every hard-muscled inch of his long legs, and a dirt-smeared denim workshirt, unbuttoned and hanging open over his smooth coppery chest. The sleeves were rolled halfway up his forearms, bits of straw clinging to the fabric, and he was wearing leather work gloves, so old and worn that the sweat-stained cuffs curled back over the rounded bones of his wrists. A beautifully worked silver buckle set with a single large square of polished turquoise glinted just below his navel, catching the sunlight with every step he took.

Ranger buckle, Victoria said to herself, identifying it without conscious effort. *Late 1800s. Probably Navajo.*

He stopped less than two feet in front of her. "Need some help, miss?" he asked softly. The cadence of his voice was almost musical.

Victoria's eyes traveled swiftly from his belt buckle, up over the flatness of his stomach and the smooth hard planes of his bare chest, to his face. She could make out the shadowed curve of his jaw and a hint of firm lips, but his eyes were hidden by the brim of his hat.

It didn't matter, she decided. Help had arrived. And such help. Who'd have thought a Greek god would be running around loose in the middle of the Arizona desert?

"Boy, do I!" Relief was evident in her voice. "I was beginning to think I'd driven into the Twilight Zone or something, and there was no one left in the world but me."

"The desert's a big place," he agreed, his eyes taking a quick inventory despite the lecture he had given himself. She wore small, creamy pearls in the lobes of her ears, a lace-trimmed something under her gauzy blouse and a perfume that smelled of night-blooming flowers and forbidden sex. He told himself to ignore it. "All this red dust and scrub growth can make it seem pretty empty and alien to someone who's not used to it." He motioned toward the open hood of the car with one gloved hand. "What's the problem?"

"I'm not real sure." Victoria lifted her elegant shoulders in a helpless little shrug and smiled up at her rescuer. It was the same smile she had used on waiters, department store clerks and household help all of her twenty-six years. *I know you can help me*, that smile said. *I have confidence in you.* It made most people want not to disappoint her.

It made the small hairs rise up on the back of John's neck. Along with a weakness for delicate builds and gorgeous legs, he also had a thing about beautiful women who thought a smile was all it took to get through life. His ex-wife had been one.

"Something's wrong with the cooling system, I think," Victoria said then, her smile fading a bit at his lack of response to it. She backed up as he came around the front of the car. "The temperature gauge has been acting up for the past twenty miles or so. It keeps climbing into the red."

He nodded to show he had heard her and pulled off one of his gloves. Stuffing it into the waistband of his jeans, he ducked his head and leaned over the engine. A small silver pendant dangled from a leather thong around his neck as he reached out to touch the radiator cap, testing it for heat.

"It's not low on water," she said as he began to unscrew the cap. "I poured over a gallon into it a little while ago."

"A gallon of what?" He tilted his head, indicating the small green bottle sitting on the air filter. A faint smile of masculine derision curved his lips. *City women.* "Fancy French soda water?"

"No, of course not." Victoria snatched the bottle out from under the hood. "I was just having a drink while I checked the engine," she explained, suppressing the urge to hide the offending bottle behind her back. "I put regular water in the radiator. From a plastic jug I brought along for just such a purpose," she added. "But I had to use it all. The engine has been overheating for a while now and—"

John nodded again without looking at her, as if she were a chattering child he wasn't really listening to, and lifted the radiator cap to check for himself.

Victoria gritted her teeth. She wasn't used to being dismissed like some dimwitted child, and she didn't like it one little bit. Even when—*especially* when—the man dismissing her was the most gorgeous hunk she'd seen in a long time. It was . . . infuriating, she decided, to be so casually disregarded by a man she found so attractive.

"It's not the hose, either," she informed him crisply as he ran his fingers along its fat black length. "I already checked it and it's okay." She tucked the owner's manual under her arm and reached out, wiggling the hose with an authoritative gesture, as if it were something she did every day. "See?"

John's hand stilled on the hose, his eyes flickering to where her arm brushed against his. "Do you mind?" he drawled, trying not to notice how pale and delicate her skin looked against the copper of his, how smooth and cool it felt. "I need room to work. And you, little lady, are in my way."

Victoria went absolutely still for a brief moment, unable to believe that he was being so condescending. So churlish. Then her chin lifted a notch, the gesture as haughty as that of an affronted queen, and she stepped back. "Pardon me."

Just pardon me all to hell, she added silently, fuming at his patronizing, superior-male manner.

Her sister-in-law, Lindsay, had warned her before she set out on this buying trip that some of the Navajos could be taciturn and occasionally even rude or hostile toward unknown Anglos. And it was understandable, she supposed, given the history between the two races. But this wasn't a case of simple racial distrust, this was an out-and-out case of rampant male chauvinism of the worst kind. Apparently Navajo men were just as likely to suffer from it as Anglos. If, in fact, he actually was a Navajo.

His heavy silver-and-turquoise belt buckle was certainly Navajo workmanship. But the little pendant charm around his neck looked more like a creation of the Hopi or Zuni tribes.

She knew that the different tribes traded freely among themselves and that it wasn't unusual to see a Navajo woman using baskets woven by her Pueblo neighbors, or a Zuni wearing a Hopi-made kachina charm. Although, she reflected, with the ongoing land dispute between the Hopi and the Navajo, it seemed unlikely that one would wear the work of the other. Still, knowing all that didn't tell her what tribe this tall, arrogant, unfriendly specimen belonged to.

Not that she wanted to know, anyway, she told herself, willing her eyes away from his big work-roughened hand as it jiggled engine parts. All she wanted was for him to fix her car so she could be on her way. If he wanted to act like an uncivilized chauvinist pig in the process, well, that was his problem, not hers.

"Here's your problem," he said, then, startling her. Victoria looked up into his shadowed face, wondering for a moment if she had spoken her thoughts out loud. He waved his hand toward the engine. "No fan belt."

Victoria turned her gaze to the engine. It took her a minute to absorb his meaning. "No fan belt? Really?"

she edged forward, the owner's manual still tucked under her arm, the bottle of Perrier in her hand, and leaned under the hood to see. "What happened to it?"

"I imagine it fell off somewhere," he said dryly. His voice had the half-amused, half-derisive tone of a man talking to a not-quite-so bright woman.

Victoria's fingers tightened on the Perrier bottle for a moment. *Temper, Victoria,* she cautioned herself. *Temper. Screaming at a man like this will do absolutely no good. He'd just put it down to typical female hysteria.* She straightened slowly and took a deep breath.

"Can you fix it?" she asked tightly, focusing her eyes on the tiny charm around his neck. She didn't trust herself to look directly at him; she wasn't sure she could keep her cool if she actually saw the smirk she had heard in his oddly musical voice.

"Depends." He lifted his shoulders in a careless shrug, and the tight mounds of his pectoral muscles rippled under his skin. "Got a spare fan belt?"

Show-off, Victoria thought derisively, and shifted her gaze to his chin. It was firm and slightly squared, with a faint cleft at its base. The mouth above it was full and sensual, the deep bow of the upper lip giving it a surprisingly tender look. With an effort, Victoria shifted her gaze again, turning her attention back to the engine.

"A spare fan belt?" she said then. "No, I don't think so, unless—" Her forehead wrinkled above the wide round lenses of her sunglasses. "Would it be part of the car's standard equipment?"

"No."

"Then I don't have a spare fan belt." She glanced upward, trying to judge the effect of her words, but his eyes were still hidden under the pulled-down brim of his hat. Just as well, she told herself. They were probably too close together and beady, as befitted a male chauvinist pig. The thought made her smile slightly; it was comforting to think that at least one thing about him wasn't Greek-god perfect. "So what now?" she asked.

"I'll have to rig up something that'll get you as far as the gas station in Chinle." He rubbed his chin with the back of his ungloved hand for a moment, thinking. "Got another belt besides the one you're wearing?" he said, pushing up the brim of his hat with his thumb.

Victoria's complacent little smile vanished. His eyes weren't close together. They weren't beady. They weren't piggy. They were, in fact, as Greek-god perfect as the rest of him. Neither brown, nor green, nor gold, they were that indefinable color known as hazel. Set at a slant above the prominent slash of his cheekbones they glittered like pale jewels against his smooth coppery skin.

It took all her suddenly scattered concentration to answer his question. "Yes, I have another belt," she said, staring up at him from behind the protection of her sunglasses. "In my luggage. But what for?"

"To use as an emergency fan belt. It'd have to be narrower than the one you've got on, though. Say an inch and a half, maybe two inches wide." His lips pursed consideringly, his eyes narrowing as they skimmed down her slim torso. "Then again . . ." He reached out and clasped her waist in both hands.

Victoria stiffened in surprise. The owner's manual slid from under her arm and dropped to the dust between their feet.

"Hey. Whoa, there." John's hands tightened, steadying her. "I'm not going to hurt you. I just wanted to measure—" The words stuck in his throat.

What he just wanted to do, he realized, was exactly what he *was* doing. Touch her. But not just the firm, warm flesh that he held between his two hands. He wanted to cup the tempting swell of her breasts in his palms. He wanted to run his fingers slowly down the length of her gorgeous legs. He wanted... John yanked his hands away from her waist as if he'd been burned.

"Never mind. It'd be too small, anyway."

"What?" Victoria's voice was hardly more than a whisper. "What would be too small?"

"Your belt. Your waist isn't any bigger than a skinny twelve-year-old's." Abruptly he bent down and retrieved the fallen manual. "Here." He shoved it into her free hand and turned away. "I'll see if I have anything in my truck I can use."

Victoria stood where she was for a moment, watching him walk away from her. Then she lifted the bottle of Perrier to her lips and took a long cooling sip, consciously stifling the urge to look down to see if his hands had actually left burn marks on the waist of her dress.

2

JOHN FOUND A NARROW LEATHER STRAP in the bed of his pickup. It was too long but he cut it down using a folding knife that he took from a toolbox behind the seat in the truck's cab. He poked a couple of holes in each end with a wooden-handled awl, then threaded a piece of rawhide twine through them to fashion a makeshift fan belt.

Victoria stood by the right fender of the car while he worked, far enough back to be out of his way but not so far that she couldn't see what he was doing under the hood. *No telling when I might have to fix the fan belt myself*, she rationalized, her eyes unconsciously following the smooth flex and coil of his muscles as he maneuvered the loose circle of leather into place. His chest, his shoulders, even his neck were corded with powerful-looking sinew and flesh that reacted to every precise, economical movement of his strong brown hands.

Victoria sighed almost regretfully. He was one of the most beautiful men she had ever laid eyes on. And it was really too bad—not to mention grossly unfair—that such a splendid example of masculine pulchritude was also such a chauvinist swine. Not unfair to her, of course. It didn't matter a fig to her, personally, that he had such outmoded ideas about women; he would fix her car and be out of her life in the next fifteen minutes. But it would matter to other women. *Lots* of other women, if she was any judge.

She lifted the Mercedes owner's manual, languidly fanning herself as she watched a bead of sweat form in the shallow valley between the smooth mounds of his pectorals. It slid slowly down his chest, trickling languorously, inch by inch, over the sculpted flatness of his stomach to finally disappear into the waistband of his dusty jeans. She tracked it with her eyes, her thumb absently rubbing up and down the side of the bottle in her hand, gathering the drops of condensation that had formed on the cool green glass.

Does he come by that body naturally, she wondered, *or does he have to work at it?*

His chest muscles coiled again, bunching into tight mounds as he pulled hard on the rawhide strings before he knotted them.

He works at it, she decided. *He must. Nobody's that perfect naturally.*

She wondered if he worked out at a health club, pumping iron like her brother Conrad, or if he'd earned his Greek-god physique with more honest labor.

Honest labor, she decided after a moment's reflection. His muscles weren't the overdeveloped kind that came from dedicated workouts with weight machines and dumbbells. Besides, she doubted that the Navajo reservation would have an organized health club of that kind. She could picture him chopping wood, though, or digging post holes or hoisting bales of hay into the back of his pickup.

He would be shirtless, of course. His bare arms and shoulders and back gleaming with the sheen of healthy exertion; his chestnut-brown hair curling damply around his ears; his strong, hard hands wrapped around the handle of an ax or a shovel or a pair of hay hooks.

She would tiptoe up behind him while he worked, she decided dreamily, and run the tip of her fingernail down the hollow of his spine. He would drop his hay hooks and turn around quickly before she could dart away. His hands—those big, warm hands—would envelop her waist, tightening as he pulled her to him. And she would laugh and slide her own hands up his arms to his shoulders, glorying in the feel of the smooth copper skin that rippled under her palms. His head would bend toward hers, his mouth— "There. That ought to hold it."

Victoria snapped out of her daydream, her eyes darting guiltily to his face. He wasn't looking at her. *Thank God!* "Is it—" Her voice came out in a squeak. She cleared her throat and tried again. "Is it fixed?"

"Temporarily." He slashed through the trailing ends of the rawhide with one swipe of the knife and tossed them into the open toolbox on the ground beside him.

"How—" Her throat was still too dry. She took a quick sip of the bubbling soda water to moisten it, hoping he hadn't noticed . . . anything. "How temporarily?"

"It'll get you as far as Chinle." The knife clicked as he pressed it closed against his jeans-clad thigh. He dropped it into the toolbox. "And I'll be right behind you in case you have any trouble," he added, lifting his gaze to her face as he reached upward with both hands for the hood of the car. His position scooped out his already concave belly, highlighting his lean, sculpted torso and the smooth, hard swell of his chest.

Victoria averted her eyes. "That really isn't necessary."

He looked at her between his upraised arms. "Yes it is. You could break down again before you get to the gas station. Watch your fingers." The hood slammed shut. "Besides, there's only one road." A ghost of that superior-male smile touched his lips for a moment. "And since we're both traveling in the same direction, I'd be following you in any case."

"Oh, yes. Of course." Victoria lifted the bottle of Perrier to her lips again. It was empty. "Well," she said briskly, turning away from him to toss it and the owner's manual into the open window on the passenger side of the car, "I guess we'd better not waste any more time, then."

"Guess not," John agreed easily, but the hairs on the back of his neck bristled at her lady-of-the-manor tone. He dropped to his haunches in front of the car and slapped the lid of the toolbox closed with the flat of his hand. *Spoiled little twit. Doesn't she know how to say thank you?* He fastened the locks with an annoyed snap, grabbed the well-worn plastic handle in one hand and stood up—just as Victoria rounded the front of the car.

His shoulder brushed against her thigh, the rough fabric of his denim shirt snagging and lifting the gauzy material of her skirt as he straightened. She gasped and took a quick step back, reaching out with both hands to push it down. The lightweight skirt billowed with the movement, fluttering like a feather on the hot air before settling around her. It was over in seconds, her modesty restored in the blink of an eye. But not before John had caught a fleeting glimpse of a slender thigh, a bare hip and the rounded curve of a firm buttock.

All she had under her skirt was a minuscule scrap of white lace and the longest, most gorgeous legs he had ever seen. *Sweet God in heaven—they must start all the way up at her waist!*

Altered images of her long bare legs and tiny lace panties began flickering through his mind with lightning speed. Different poses. Different positions. Different settings. But all with the same theme. He tried to ignore them, telling himself sternly to think of something else. Now was *not* the time to be indulging in erotic fantasies. And she was most certainly *not* the woman. But try telling that to his body; it was reacting as if she had stripped naked and offered herself to him.

"Sorry about that," he mumbled, gesturing at her skirt with a lift of the toolbox. "I hope I didn't get you dirty."

"No . . . no, it's fine." Head down, Victoria brushed the side of her skirt with trembling hands. "Just a little dust, that's all. It comes right off. See?" She looked up at him from under her lashes, a small nervous smile on her lips. Their eyes met.

For Victoria it was like looking into the golden-hued eyes of a mountain lion. A *hungry* mountain lion, just waiting to see which way his dinner would run before he pounced on it.

For John it was as frustrating as hell. She was still wearing her sunglasses. God, he hated sunglasses! He wanted to reach out and slide them off of her elegant little nose, to see if her eyes were as soft and inviting as her glossy red mouth. And then he wanted to taste . . .

City woman, he reminded himself sternly, as if the words were an incantation that would keep him from acting on those wants.

"Well, let's get a move on," he said gruffly, stepping back to allow her to precede him around to the driver's side of the car. "I've got better things to do than stand around in the middle of the road all day."

Victoria nodded, too bemused for the moment to take offense at his tone. She walked just past the car door, then turned, waiting for him to open it for her.

City woman, he thought again, reaching for the door handle. *Useless as teats on a ram.* "Get in."

Victoria's murmured "Thank you" was barely audible. She settled gingerly into the driver's seat, bunching the fabric of her skirt under her thighs to shield them from the burning heat of the red-leather interior.

"All settled?" John's voice was a low rasp. She had leaned forward, hunching her shoulders as she arranged her skirt, and the resulting gap at the front of her wide-necked blouse afforded him a clear view of the lacy white . . . whatever it was that she was wearing next to her skin. *She certainly doesn't believe in wasting a lot of material on her underclothes.* The thought did absolutely nothing to cool his body's response to her. He shut the car door with a firm push.

"Chinle is about eight or ten miles straight down the highway." He put his free hand on the roof of the car, bending his knees both to speak to her through the open window and in an unconscious effort to hide his reaction to her inadvertent display of flesh. "Keep it under fifty and don't use the air conditioner, and you'll be fine."

Eyes straight ahead, Victoria nodded, not trusting herself to look at him. Seated the way she was, with him standing by the car, his bare stomach would be just about eye level. She didn't think she could take staring into his navel right now; her breathing was erratic enough already. She started the engine, revving it a bit as if she were impatient to be off.

John straightened and took his hand from the car. "I'll be right behind you if you have any problems," he said tightly. "So just pull over if it starts acting up."

Victoria nodded again. "Okay, fine. And . . . and thank you," she added belatedly, turning her head to look at him. It was a mistake. It wasn't his belly button she was eye-to-eye with. It was his lean jeans-clad hips. And they were— It was— Her eyes widened at the sight.

Good Lord, the buttons of his fly are about to give way under the strain of his . . . Victoria shied away from the thought. Her head whipped forward, her hands tightening on the leather-wrapped steering wheel. An unaccustomed blush stained her elegant cheekbones.

"Well, uh, thank you for your, umm, help," she managed, staring straight ahead. She put the car into gear, stepped on the gas and shot out onto the blacktop highway. A small cloud of dust and gravel rose from beneath her rear tires.

John stood still for a second, staring at the rapidly receding car. *Spoiled, ungrateful little twit,* he thought, and turned toward his pickup. The fabric of his jeans pinched him as he walked, and he passed a hand over his fly, pulling at the tight denim to ease the restriction. A grin tugged at the corners of his sensual mouth. *Goddamned gorgeous little twit, though.*

With quick but unhurried movements, he stowed the toolbox behind his seat, tossed his hat onto the passenger side of the cab and slid behind the wheel of the truck. The engine rumbled softly, gravel crunching under the tires as he steered back onto the highway.

The Mercedes was already little more than a white blur on the road ahead of him. She might be holding it to fifty, but he doubted it. *Drives like the proverbial bat out of hell,* he thought, accelerating until he was exceeding the speed limit almost by twenty miles an hour. Somehow it didn't surprise him. Women like her—driving cars like that—usually did. And then they used their thousand-watt smiles to try to charm their way out of the tickets that inevitably resulted.

He eased up on the gas pedal, letting the truck settle back to a more reasonable speed. No sense wasting fuel chasing her. If she broke down again, she'd have to stop. And wait. It'd probably do her good. A woman like that had probably had to wait for damned little in her life; her barely concealed impatience to be on her way told him that. It gave John a curious sense of satisfaction to think that she might have to wait for him.

Victoria covered two miles before her blush receded and then another two before she realized that she was exceeding the fifty miles an hour her rescuer had advised as safe for the makeshift fan belt. She let up on the accelerator, slowing the Mercedes, and glanced into the rearview mirror. He was behind her, just as he had said he would be, his truck slowly closing the gap she had created with her excess speed. It made her feel as if she were being chased.

"The fan belt, Victoria," she mumbled to herself, fighting the urge to speed up again. "Remember the fan belt." The last thing she needed was to break down and be forced to accept his help again.

The man was pure Neanderthal—that's what he was, she fumed silently. A rude, arrogant Neanderthal with . . . with overly macho instincts. Running around with his chest hanging out like that. Showing off his muscles. Sweating just enough to make them gleam. And no doubt expecting her to drool all over him.

Which, to her undying embarrassment, was exactly what she had done. Had he seen her doing it?

Victoria lifted a hand from the steering wheel to brush at the hair flying around her face. Oh, yes, he'd seen her doing it all right. How else would you explain his state of obvious arousal? A man certainly didn't get that way just standing around in the hot sun.

He'd probably planned for it to happen, she decided, conveniently channeling all her whirling emotions into feminine outrage at his macho strutting. *He probably hoped that I'd see it and be so overcome that I'd fall all over him.*

A sudden graphic picture formed in her mind of the two of them lying on the front seat of his pickup, their clothes half off and tangled around them, their passion-slicked bodies straining toward fulfillment.

She shook her head, silently denying the fantasy— and the rush of heat that had pooled between her thighs.

"Forget it," she said out loud. "Just forget it. Nothing happened. The car's fine. There's a gas station up ahead. You never have to see or speak to the man again."

She slowed the car, flicking on her signal as she turned left into the service station, and put her hand out the window, thumb and forefinger circled to show that everything was okay now; he could drive on and leave her.

But he didn't.

She could see him in her side mirror, slowing the truck to turn in behind her.

Victoria stifled the urge to slip under the steering wheel. It wouldn't do any good, anyway, she told herself. He'd just stick his head in the car window, his lips turned up in that aggravating superior-male smirk of his, and haul her up off the floorboards as if she were some feeble-minded child. His hands against her arms would be hard and brown, and they would touch her with...

Smarten up, Victoria! Her hands on the steering wheel showed white at the knuckles. *You don't want that man's hands anywhere near you!*

"Fill 'er up?"

Victoria turned her head. A service-station attendant peered into her window, his round face shaded by a Dodgers' baseball cap, his expression inquiring and helpful but unsmiling.

Victoria unclenched her fingers. "No, I don't need any gas, thank you," she said shakily, wondering if it were against tradition for Navajo men to smile—or if it was something about her that made them so solemn. "Well, actually, I guess I do. Need gas, I mean. But that's not my main problem." She glanced in the rearview mirror. He was standing inside the open door of his truck, one hand braced on the doorframe as he reached across the seat for his cowboy hat. *Ignore him.* She looked at the station attendant. "My main problem is the fan belt. It's broken."

"Broke, ma'am?"

"Yes. It—" The door of his truck banged shut. *Ignore it, Victoria.* "It . . ." Her eyes wandered to the rearview mirror. He was walking toward her car, the sun glinting off his belt buckle with every easy rolling step. He was even with her rear bumper. He—

"Ma'am?"

She snapped her attention back to the station attendant. "My fan belt fell off somewhere."

"You don't have a fan belt in your engine?"

"No. I mean, yes, I do. But it's not a real fan belt, it's, ah . . ." *Take charge, Victoria. Stop acting like such a spineless wimp!* "Wait a minute." She reached down and popped the hood release. "I'll show you."

A large brown hand settled over her door handle, pulling it open before she could do it herself. "What the lady is trying to say, Willie—" he reached down and cupped her elbow, lifting her out of the driver's seat as if she were a helpless doll "—is that she's operating with a jerry-rigged fan belt and she needs a new one." He glanced down at her, his eyes once again shaded by the pulled down brim of his straw cowboy hat. "Isn't that right, little lady?"

"Yes, that's right," Victoria agreed tightly, looking up at him with a polite, frosty smile on her face. *If he calls me "little lady" just one more time . . .* She eased her elbow out of his hand, turning her back on him to speak directly to the station attendant. It was a little move she had perfected as a debutante to quell overeager suitors. Performing it now made her feel in control again. *There,* she thought. *Take that, you arrogant, muscle-bound swine.*

"My fan belt apparently fell off quite a way back," she said to the station attendant. "And this—" her hesitation was slight but telling "—gentleman was kind enough to stop and ah . . ."

"Jerry-rig it," the "gentleman" supplied.

"Yes, jerry-rig it. Thank you," she said, without looking at him. She smiled her thousand-watt I-know-you-can-help-me smile at the station attendant. "Do you think you can fix it properly?"

He lifted his Dodgers' cap by the bill, wiped his shirt sleeve across his forehead and settled the cap back into place before answering. "Well, I dunno," he said slowly, his eyes sweeping the length of the flashy little car. "That's not exactly a Chevy you're drivin'." He looked up at the man standing behind her. "Whaddaya think, John? Is there a Mercedes dealer in Flagstaff?"

"Don't know offhand. Probably. If there isn't one there you could always call Phoenix."

"Yeah, Phoenix for sure. Might have to wait two, maybe th—"

"Excuse me . . . Willie, isn't it?" Victoria's voice, soft, low and icy broke between them.

"Yes, ma'am. Willie Salt."

"Well, Mr. Salt, believe it or not I am entirely capable of handling a discussion about the repair of my car myself. I don't need a third person to take care of it for me." She was being rude, she knew, but enough was enough. "Am I making myself clear?"

Willie Salt nodded.

"Good." She turned to the man standing behind her. "As for your Mr. . . . ?"

"John'll do."

Victoria nodded. "John, then." She leaned over, reaching sideways into the open window of her car, and scooped her purse up off the seat. "I appreciate your taking the time and effort to stop and help me, John," she said, rummaging in her purse. "And I'd like to offer you a tangible expression of my gratitude." She extended her hand. "Thank you."

John didn't even glance at the ten-dollar bill she offered. "No thanks are necessary."

"Take it, please. I'd like to repay you for the cost of the leather strap at least."

"The strap was nothing. Just a piece of scrap material," he said, fighting down a quick surge of anger. No, not anger, he decided. Irritation. Annoyance. The little twit didn't even realize she was insulting him with her offer of money. He had only done for her what any other Navajo would have done; his people prided themselves on their hospitality to visitors.

"You're sure?" Victoria urged.

"Quite sure."

"Well, then." She put the money back in her purse and held out her hand, empty this time and open.

John looked down at it for a second, the space of a heartbeat only, then reached out and enclosed it in his own. It was soft and small in his but surprisingly strong. Her grip was as firm as any young man's.

"Thank you for your help, John. I appreciate it." She withdrew her hand from his with a brisk there-that's-done gesture and turned to Willie Salt.

He had been dismissed. By an expert. *The little twit dismissed me as casually as if I were her butler.* He couldn't let her get away with it. He reached out a long arm and tapped her on the shoulder. "Little lady?"

Victoria's head snapped around, a line of annoyance marring the smooth forehead above her sunglasses. "Yes? What is it?"

John grinned. She sounded like a schoolteacher. An irritated schoolteacher. "I'll be at the café across the street when you need me."

"Need you?" Her chin lifted. "I won't need you."

"Oh, I think you will." He turned from her then and sauntered back to his pickup. Out of the corner of her eye Victoria watched him back up and drive out of the gas station, across the street and into the gravel parking lot of the Canyon Café.

Twenty minutes later, from her perch atop her suitcase next to Willie Salt's soft-drink machine, she watched him drive back. He pulled to a stop in front of her, leaned across the seat and opened the passenger door. "Need a ride, little lady?"

For a moment Victoria considered telling him just exactly what he could do with his ride. But just for a moment. She was hot. And sweaty. She wanted an aspirin. And a bath. And a turkey club sandwich with an extra-crisp dill pickle and a tall, cool glass of iced tea.

But Willie Salt had already informed her that it would be a couple of hours yet before he'd be free to give her a lift to the motel. It would be three days, at least, before a fan belt arrived from Phoenix so she could drive herself. And Chinle didn't have a taxi service.

She eyed the man inside the cab of the pickup. "Does that thing have air conditioning?"

He grinned, showing strong white teeth and a faint dimple in his left cheek. "Sure thing, little lady."

Victoria gritted her teeth and got in.

3

VICTORIA LOOKED AT HER WATCH again, uncrossed her legs and stood up. Five quick, impatient steps brought her to the reception desk of the Thunderbird Lodge. "Are you sure no one's left a message for me?" she asked the smooth-faced Navajo woman behind the counter. "Victoria Dillon?"

"No, Miss Dillon, I'm sorry. There have been no messages for you. There are no phones in the canyon, you know, so someone must come," the receptionist said. A shy conciliatory smile curved her lips. "If you'd like to wait in your room or on the patio in front of the gift shop," she suggested, gesturing toward the glass-paned doors that led outside. "It's nice under the trees, and I'll make sure your message gets to you as soon as it's delivered."

Victoria shook her head; she didn't want to chance missing her meeting with Maria Redcloud because somebody couldn't find her when she—or a message—finally arrived. "I'll wait here, thanks," she said, turning away from the reception counter with a sigh and a silent admonition to be patient.

She wasn't dealing with the hustle and bustle of Phoenix, she reminded herself. Her sister-in-law, Lindsay, had specifically warned her about the difficulties of communicating with the residents of the

Canyon de Chelly before she left on this buying trip. But that didn't make it any easier to deal with. It was after ten o'clock already, and business was business. Or should be.

You'd think Mrs. Redcloud would have found a way to get a message to me by now, she thought, plopping herself back down in her chair, *even if she'd had to send it by Indian runner or carrier pigeon or something.* She picked up a magazine from the low table in front of her and began flipping idly through it, her mind focused inward as she recalled her sister-in-law's words of advice.

"Life moves at a slower pace in Navajoland. Much slower," Lindsay had warned. "So relax and enjoy it."

Easy for Lindsay to say, she thought irritably. Lindsay wasn't—

Victoria straightened in the chair, the explanation for the lack of communication suddenly as clear as the blazing summer sky. The magazine fell closed. *Of course! Lindsay!*

The reason there was no message for Victoria was because Maria Redcloud was expecting Lindsay. Lindsay was the Indian-arts expert. She was the one who made the long, hot drive from Phoenix to the Navajo reservation every summer to buy handmade rugs and blankets for the family department store's Indian Arts Boutique. But Lindsay was pregnant this summer. With twins. And Victoria, restless and at loose ends since her divorce eight months ago, had volunteered to make the trip in her sister-in-law's place. She tossed the magazine back onto the table and hurried toward the recep-

tion desk. "Do you **have** a message for Lindsay Cullen?"
she asked, sure that there would be one.

But the receptionist wasn't paying any attention to
her. Instead, her black eyes were focused just beyond
the glass-paned doors that opened to the outside. And
there was a smile—a real smile—curving up the corners of her generous mouth. Curious, Victoria turned
her head to follow the direction of the Indian woman's
gaze.

It was him. The white knight with the Greek-god
physique and the condescending manner. And he
looked just as Greek-god perfect in clean jeans and a
buttoned shirt as he had yesterday all dirty and bare
chested. No wonder the receptionist was smiling. If she
didn't know firsthand what a patronizing swine he was,
Victoria might have been tempted to smile herself. Un-
knowingly, she licked her lips instead.

Whatever his attitude toward women, he was a prime
example of virile beauty. Standing there in the morning sun with his hat pulled low over his forehead and
the Western-cut yoke of his pale blue shirt making his
shoulders look impossibly broad, he was enough to
make even the most die-hard feminist's heart beat
faster. He stood with one knee slightly bent, his leather-
gloved hands resting lightly on his narrow hips, the
sleeves of his blue shirt rolled up to expose muscular,
copper-hued forearms, listening attentively to whatever the teenager in the maid's uniform was saying to
him. He shook his head once, laughing, then reached
out and squeezed the girl's shoulder. She pursed her lips
and shrugged, flapping her hand in pretended dis-

missal. He laughed again and chucked her under the chin with his gloved fist, then turned toward the lobby.

Cradle-robber, Victoria sneered, unconsciously admiring the lazy, loose-hipped way he walked. He had the unhurried, sensual swagger of a confident man, that unconsciously sexy roll of the hips that told her he was sure of himself and his place in the world, that measured stride that said he knew exactly where he was going and how to get there. It wasn't until he lifted his hand and pushed in on the door that she realized that his easy, unhurried walk was bringing him inside the lobby.

Victoria turned back to the receptionist. "Do you have a message for Lindsay Cullen?" she said again, her voice gone unaccountably breathless.

But the Indian woman was still looking past her. "Good morning, John," she said to the man who had just come in. Dimples showed on either side of her wide smile. "What can I do for you?"

Victoria heard his boot heels click against the floor as he crossed the lobby behind her. Long, unhurried, ground-eating strides. She shifted sideways, edging around a tall, potted cactus, wishing suddenly that she hadn't been quite so outspoken in her opinion of his manners when he'd dropped her off at the lodge yesterday afternoon.

Not that he hadn't deserved every cutting word, of course, she thought, pretending an interest in the colorful brochures displayed on the counter. He'd gone and called her "little lady" just one too many times with that half-amused look in his hazel eyes and that condescending tone in his voice, and she'd given in to the urge to tell him exactly what he could do with his male superiority, slamming the door of his truck to drive the point home. Still, she thought now, she might have managed to be a tad more diplomatic if she'd known she was going to run into him again.

"Mornin', Ruth," he said, the almost musical cadence of his low voice floating through the air like warm smoke from a campfire. "I'm looking for one of your guests. Lindsay Cullen. I've got a message for her from Grandmother. You seen her around?"

Victoria's head snapped up, her fingers tightening on the brochure in her hand. *A message? For Lindsay?*

The receptionist was shaking her head. "There's no Lindsay Cullen registered."

"You sure? Grandmother was supposed to meet her here this morning."

Grandmother? Victoria thought, a horrible suspicion beginning to form in her mind. *His* grandmother was supposed to meet Lindsay?

The Indian woman flipped through a card file. "No, she's not here, John. Sorry."

"Well, darn it all. I wonder where the hell she is. Grandmother wanted me to fetch her out to the canyon."

Victoria sighed, silently accepting the inevitable, and laid the brochure back on the counter, carefully aligning it on the pile she had taken it from. "Excuse me," she said. They didn't seem to hear her. She stepped around the cactus plant. "Ah, excuse me," she said more loudly.

Both heads turned toward her.

"I'm Lindsay Cullen." She spoke directly to the receptionist. It was easier than looking at the tall man standing beside her. She knew he'd be smirking, thinking she'd been deliberately hiding from him behind that damned cactus plant—which she had. "That is, I'm not Lindsay, I'm her sister-in-law, but I'm here in her place. To see Mrs. Redcloud," she added, still not looking at the man she could sense was staring intently at her, "about the rugs and blankets and things."

The receptionist frowned.

"I've been hanging around here, waiting for a message?" Victoria prompted, her inflection making it an almost question.

"Oh, yes. Yes." Comprehension dawned in the woman's eyes. She looked up at John. "This lady's been waiting for a message since a little after nine. I guess she's the one you're looking for."

Steeling herself, Victoria turned to meet the Greek-god's gaze.

"Well, well, well," drawled John, pushing the brim of his hat up with his thumb. A vagrant lock of brown hair tumbled over his forehead. "If it isn't the little lady with no fan belt. I didn't see you standing there when I first came in," he said, his hazel eyes running over her appreciatively.

She was dressed all in white again: a crisp, sleeveless white dress that made her smooth, tanned skin look like honey; a wide white leather belt that wrapped snugly around her ridiculously tiny waist; strappy white sandals that fastened around her elegant ankles and left ten glossy red toenails bare; a white comb that held her silky black hair up and back on the left side. She looked as cool and fresh and inviting as a tall glass of sparkling well water at high noon on the hottest day of the year. He wondered if she were wearing those scanty scraps of white lace underneath her ladylike little dress.

"So," he said, his eyes narrowing as he remembered those brief glimpses of her lace-covered flesh—and the way those glimpses had made him feel. He'd spent an uncomfortable night dreaming of little else. "How're you feeling after your— What was it you called it?" He arched an eyebrow, wanting to bother her as much as she bothered him. "A 'thoroughly unpleasant experience at the hands of a caveman,' wasn't it?"

Victoria's chin lifted. "I believe 'Neanderthal' was the word I used," she said, refusing to be intimated by his slow, heated perusal of her.

"Yeah, Neanderthal—that was it." He smiled and leaned back, propping an elbow on the counter behind him as if he couldn't care less what she'd called him— although it'd made him damned mad yesterday. But that was yesterday. And he wasn't one to hold a grudge. "I don't believe I've ever been called a Neanderthal before," he said easily.

"Really?" she murmured, determined not to be charmed. "I find that hard to believe." Her eyes held his with a level, challenging look, the barest hint of answering humor in their depths despite her determination. They were dark, bittersweet-chocolate eyes, set off by thick inky-black lashes that matched her hair, framed by arched black eyebrows, subtly made up to take full advantage of their faintly exotic shape.

A spitfire's eyes in spite of the icy stare, John thought, and found himself wondering what they'd look like glazed and burning with passion, or soft and glowing in the aftermath of love. They'd shoot sparks, he decided, and then they'd smolder like embers in the aftermath.

Their eyes continued to hold for a few seconds more; hers full of cool, wary challenge; his brimming with masculine speculation; both of them teasing around the edges of unwilling sexual heat and humor. And then, suddenly, humor won. It had to. They couldn't very well lunge at each other there in the quiet lobby of the Thunderbird Lodge. They told themselves they didn't even want to.

"You gonna start calling me nasty names again?" John said lazily.

Victoria's low laugh bubbled out then, taking her temper with it. "No, not this time." She smiled up at him, on her way to being charmed in spite of herself. "Shall we start over?"

"Start over?"

"From the beginning." She held out her right hand. "I'm Victoria Dillon, Lindsay's sister-in-law," she said formally, "and I'm pleased to make your acquaintance."

John straightened and stripped off his glove. "John Redcloud." He took her hand in his. "I'm pleased to meet you, too, Miss Dillon."

"Victoria, please," she said.

They dropped hands quickly, both of them denying the quick, hot flash of feeling that sizzled between them at the casual touch of palm to palm.

Spoiled city woman, John told himself sternly, trying not to speculate on what feelings longer, more intimate contact might call forth.

Arrogant swine, Victoria reminded herself, silently denying that she had any interest in how his hand might feel on another part of her anatomy.

"Well, umm—" John cleared his throat. "We'd better get a move on. Grandmother's waiting." He nodded a farewell to the receptionist. "See you around, Ruth."

"Tell Grandmother I'll drop up later this afternoon," the woman responded. "I've got that case of French pickles she wanted."

"I'll tell her."

"Your sister?" Victoria asked, falling into step beside him as they walked across the lobby.

"Cousin." He pulled open the glass-paned door, stepping back to let Victoria go ahead of him. "Second or third removed, I think," he said, automatically tugging down the brim of his hat to shade his eyes as they stepped into the sun. "Her mother is my grandmother's daughter by marriage."

"Daughter by marriage?" Victoria paused just outside the doorway, half turning to look up at him. A breath of air feathered her skirt against his legs. Pristine, airy white brushed against the rough denim of his jeans. Both of them remembered the instant the previous day when the rough fabric of his dirty workshirt had lifted her dress. Victoria swallowed and moved away. "Is that the same as a daughter-in-law?"

"More or less." He pulled the door shut behind them with a bit more force than necessary. "The Navajo are traditionally a matrilineal society," he explained, trying not to think of the tiny bit of white lace she was probably wearing under her dress right now. "A groom usually moves in with his bride's family, and we trace our descent through the female line."

Victoria nodded, falling into step beside him, careful not to walk too close as they moved across a small landscaped area between the lobby and the gift shop. "Yes, I remember reading that somewhere. And Lindsay mentioned it when she was filling me in on what to expect."

"Ah, yes. The absent Lindsay. What happened to her that she couldn't come herself?"

"Impending motherhood." Victoria held her hands way out in front of her stomach. "Twins. She just found out there were two of them a couple of weeks ago, and my brother Conrad—he's Lindsay's husband—decided he didn't want her driving all over Arizona by herself."

"So he's letting you drive all over Arizona by yourself instead."

Victoria slanted him a warning look out of the corner of her eye. "No one's *letting* me do anything."

He smiled at her tone. "A real liberated woman, huh?"

"Yes," she said forcefully, and then added, "Something you obviously know very little about."

"Oh, I don't know about that, little lady. I've—" He broke off suddenly as Victoria came to a dead stop. "Hey, I'm sorry," he said, holding up both hands, palms out, as if to ward off a blow, although she had made no move at all to hit him. *But if looks could kill,* he thought, grinning.

Victoria glared at him.

He wiped the grin off his face. "Really, I'm sorry," he said contritely. "I know you don't like to be called that. It just slipped out, kinda natural-like. And I apologize. I really do." He shrugged, smiling at her like a small boy trying to appease his angry mother. "Forgive me."

For the second time that morning, Victoria struggled to hide an answering smile. Such obvious male chauvinism was nothing to smile at, even if the chauvinist was the best-looking man in six states. Still, she couldn't expect him to break what was probably the habit of a lifetime in one day, could she? "Yes, of course I forgive you," she said, trying to be fair.

His smile widened with triumph.

On the other hand, he shouldn't be allowed to have it all his own way, either. "Just don't do it again," she said sternly.

"I'll try. I really will. But . . ."

"But what?" she asked warily.

"It'll be awfully hard." A sly, devilish smile curved his lips. "You're beautiful when you're angry."

Victoria groaned and turned away. "I can't believe you really said that," she sputtered, laughing in spite of herself. Really, the man was impossible. Impossibly charming. Impossibly good-looking. Impossibly sexy. She was halfway to the gift shop before she realized that he hadn't fallen into step beside her.

She turned around. He was standing with his fists on his hips, an appreciative half smile quirking up the corners of his mouth, watching her. At least she thought he was watching her; his eyes were hidden in the shadow of his hat. "Well?" she said, trying to ignore what that little smile, that unseen stare, did to her insides.

"Well, what?"

"Aren't you going to take me to your grandmother?"

"Sure. But my grandmother's not in the gift shop."

"Then why were we walking this way?" she demanded, exasperated.

"I wasn't walking that way," he pointed out, the very voice of reason. "You were."

"Because you were walking that— Oh, never mind!" She threw up her hands and started back toward him. "All right. Enough of this fooling around. Take me to your grandmother. Now."

He shook his head, his eyes drawn to the gentle lift and sway of her breasts under the white dress. She wasn't wearing a bra. "You'll have to change your clothes first."

"Change my clothes? Why?" She looked down at herself then back up at him, her head tilted back so that she could see under the brim of his hat. "What's the matter with my clothes?"

Arrogant little twit, he thought, admiring the aggressive thrust of her chin. It made him want to bring her down a peg. It also made him want to haul her up against him and kiss her into submission. *Not a good idea*, he warned himself. He moved a step closer, anyway.

Victoria held her ground. "Well?" she demanded, all but tapping her foot.

"You sure do fire up real easy," he said, ignoring her question. "It makes your eyes go all sparkly and…" He paused for a long moment, his gaze probing hers. Her eyes were nearly black, narrowed against the sunlight as she looked up at him. Her mouth, pursed in impatience, was lush and inviting. He wondered if it would taste as good as it looked.

"And what?" she prodded, knowing she shouldn't. But his eyes had gone all golden and hungry, and she couldn't resist the temptation.

"Hot," he said, low.

Victoria felt herself flush. Hot. Oh, yes, she felt hot. And flustered. And something else she didn't think it was wise to put a name to. Something she could read clearly in the amber depths of his eyes. "That's all men like you ever think about, isn't it?" Meant to be a stinging reprimand, the words were an invitation—and a challenge.

"What?" He lifted his hand and brushed his fingertip over her lashes. "Your eyes?"

She swayed toward him slightly, her lids drifting closed under his feather-light touch. "No, se—" She caught herself before she said it. Sex. It was what *she* was thinking about. What she'd been thinking about since the day before when he'd leaned over the engine of her car, all gleaming and bare chested and... Her eyes flew open. *What the hell's the matter with you, Victoria?* She pulled herself upright with a jerk.

But it was too late.

Instinctively, before he could even think to tell himself not to, John reached out to bring her back. His hands—big, calloused, hard—closed over her bare arms, lifting her to him. His head bent, the brim of his hat casting a shadow over her startled face. His mouth covered hers.

Victoria stiffened and gasped, her hands automatically lifting to push him away. But his tongue slipped between her open lips, hot and sweet, and her hands, when they touched the hard wall of his chest, lost all will to resist. Her head fell back under the bruising pressure of his kiss.

My God, she thought, standing there, acquiescent and accepting under the onslaught of his mouth. Where had all this come from? This sudden, overwhelming hunger? This searing heat that had nothing to do with the sun overhead? She was humming—*throbbing*— with needs and desires she hadn't felt since... Since never, she realized dazedly. She'd never felt like this before. Never, ever. She wanted it to go on forever.

But then, suddenly, his mouth lifted from hers, his hands let go of her arms, and it was over.

"Well, now that we've got that out of the way," he said, his voice husky, "I guess we'd better get a move on."

Victoria couldn't move. *Out of the way?* She blinked once, like a child just waking up. What did he mean, *out of the way?*

"Grandmother's waiting," he said tersely.

His grandmother, yes. She was supposed to meet with his grandmother about... something. "I have to change my clothes first," she said. It was the only thing she could think of that made any sense. She took a half step away from him, then stopped. "What should I change into?"

"Jeans, if you own such a thing." His voice was gruff, almost angry, but she didn't notice.

"Yes, I brought a pair of jeans with me," she said as if clothes were the only thing on her mind. "Two pairs."

"Fine." He spit the word out between clenched teeth. "You go change, and I'll meet you out in front of the gift shop."

"Okay," she agreed, turning toward her room.

"Try not to take all day about it!" he hollered after her.

"I won't," she said without even turning around.

John stood there watching her until the closing door of her room cut her off from his sight. Then, turning on his heel, he stomped off, enraged by her total lack of response—and his own overwhelming lack of restraint.

He hadn't meant to kiss her at all, he fumed, shaking his head at his own stupidity. She was exactly the kind of woman that he promised himself never to get involved with again. And yet, somehow, he'd suddenly found himself all lathered up like some kid with his first girl. Thirty-three years old, and he'd been that close— *that close*—to exploding right then and there! From one damned kiss! And she just stood there, cool as you please, the only thing on her mind what she should wear. *Damned spoiled, superficial city woman!*

4

VICTORIA WAS HALFWAY into her jeans before any emotion besides confusion could penetrate her dazed mind. And then it was anger that surfaced first. Anger at his macho, masculine presumption—grabbing her like that, as if it were his god-given right to kiss any woman he wanted to! Anger, too, at her helpless, heated response—when all he'd done was kiss her.

"Big deal," she said aloud, jerking up the zipper of her jeans with no thought to the frailty of the lace panties and soft skin beneath. "You've been kissed before."

But not like that.

Not so that it was all she could do to keep her knees from buckling. Not so that her blood heated and her body yearned. Not so that her lips still carried the taste of him, ten minutes after the fact.

She ran her tongue over them, then shook her head, denying her reaction, refusing to dwell on her overwhelming, unnerving response to that brief kiss. It was easier, more satisfying, to be angry at the lack of his.

"Now that we've got that out of the way," he'd said, as if kissing her was something he'd been mildly curious about. And then, when his curiosity had been satisfied, he'd let her go as if they'd done nothing more intimate than shake hands.

No, that wasn't quite true. It had been more than curiosity that had prompted him to kiss her. It had been the male urge to dominate. He'd been annoyed at her; ticked off because she'd dared to challenge him, and he'd reacted like the overly macho type he was and tried to overwhelm her with a kiss. The Neanderthal.

Well, it hadn't worked. She wasn't overwhelmed. Not even the least little bit. *Well, okay*, she admitted grudgingly, a tiny, unwilling smile tugging at the corner of her mouth as she sat down on the bed to tie her tennis shoes, *maybe a* little *bit*.

But, hey, he was a good kisser. Maybe one of the best. She was certainly woman enough to appreciate a kisser of his caliber when they were lip to lip. For a brief moment—a very brief moment!—she had even responded to him. Nothing earthshaking in that, she reassured herself. It was, in fact, an entirely normal reaction. No big deal. Certainly nothing to waste any more time and emotion thinking about.

Her equilibrium restored, Victoria slid her big round sunglasses onto her nose and stepped out into the day. For once in her life she had a real job to do, she reminded herself, hurrying across the hard, sunbaked ground to the gift shop. An interesting job. And no muscled, macho Greek god was going to distract her from it.

So where was he?

There was a whole group of people milling around in front of the gift shop when she got there. Fifteen or so adults and as many children, some sitting on lawn chairs on the flagstone patio, some milling around the entrance to the gift shop, most of them lined up to board the big six-wheel open-topped sightseeing vehicle that would take them on a guided tour of the canyon. But no jeans-clad, cowboy-hatted Greek god. Maybe he'd gone inside to get out of the heat while he waited for her. Victoria slipped through the congestion at the door and ducked inside the building. It was cool and shadowed, dim enough so that she had to take off her sunglasses to see clearly.

But she didn't see John.

"Would you like to buy a ticket for the canyon tour, miss?" a young Indian girl asked helpfully as Victoria stood there looking around. "We have both half-day and whole-day excursions."

"No, thank you. I'm looking for John Redcloud. He said he'd meet me here in front of the gift shop. This is the gift shop, isn't it?" she asked, her glance skimming quickly over the rich array of Indian arts and crafts that were displayed.

"Yes, but John isn't here. You might check down by the corral, though. His truck was parked there earlier."

"The corral?"

"It's down the drive a little way." The Indian girl came to the door to show her. "Right over there," she said, pointing. "Just on the other side of those trees."

Victoria nodded. "Thank you." She slipped her sunglasses back on and headed in the direction the girl had pointed, making a concerted effort to tamp down her rising annoyance. He'd told her not to take all day about it when she'd gone to change clothes, as if she were one of those ditzy women who spent an hour just deciding what dress to wear, and then he wasn't where he said he'd be. She could see his pickup truck, parked in the shade of a leafy cottonwood, but no John. Her brow furrowed above the sunglasses. Where was he?

And then, suddenly, all her annoyance disappeared as she caught sight of the corral and the horses. Most of them were run-of-the-mill riding-stable horses; safe, solid animals who could be depended on not to willingly move any faster than a slow trot. Three or four of them showed promise of more spirit. One was a real beauty.

A gleaming bay mare, showing more than a trace of Arabian ancestry in her wedge-shaped head and deep chest, danced restlessly up and down the length of the corral fence. Her black mane and tail streamed out behind her, her wide nostrils flaring as she breathed in the rich scents of the hot June day.

"Oh, you beauty, you," Victoria crooned, climbing onto the lowest rung of the fence. Leaning over, she held out her hand, palm up. "Come here, beauty. Come here."

The horse approached with a mincing sideways step, wheeled away with a nervous snort, then pranced back, her neck arched as she reached to sniff the offered hand.

"Come on. Come to me," Victoria coaxed softly. "I won't hurt you." The velvet nose just touched Victoria's fingertips. Warm breath blew across her palm. Victoria held perfectly still, letting the mare smell her. "Atta girl. Come closer. I won't hurt you." The mare took a step closer, lipping her palm for the treat that wasn't there. Victoria turned her hand and stroked the velvety-soft muzzle of the horse. "Sorry, girl," she apologized, reaching up to scratch the animal between the eyes. "I haven't got anything for you."

"Here, try this." A strong brown hand appeared over Victoria's shoulder. The horse shied away at the new voice, her mane flying as she tossed her head. John dropped the half apple he was holding into Victoria's hand. "Oh, come on, Scarlett," he chided when the horse continued to snort and shake her head. "Quit being such a flirt and take it."

The horse pranced back. "Scarlett?" Victoria asked, laughing softly as the mare lipped the apple from her palm and then crowded against the fence, looking for more.

John grinned. He'd cooled down in the last fifteen minutes. Not much, but some. Enough so that he could look at her without wanting to put his hands around her beautiful neck and squeeze. "You don't think it suits her?" He gave the animal the other half of the apple, then rubbed her nose as she chomped it.

Victoria took another look at the dark, long-lashed eyes, the arched neck, the deep, gleaming red coat. "To a T," she said. "Is she yours?"

John nodded. "Picked her up at auction four years ago. She came as a package deal with her mother." He scanned the other horses in the corral for a moment. "That roan over there."

Victoria looked where he pointed. The roan mare was one of the solid, dependable-looking horses. Nice enough but nothing special. "Her sire must have been something else."

"Must have," John agreed, pushing Scarlett's head aside when she butted against him in silent demand. "I take it you know something about horses?"

"Something." Victoria climbed another rung of the fence as she spoke, then turned and sat, balancing easily on the top rail. "I have an Arabian of my own. Ali." She patted Scarlett's neck, reaching up to caress the animal's ears. "I ride almost every day when I'm home."

"Would you like to ride now?"

"Now?" Her hand stilled on the mare's red hide. "But I thought— I mean, isn't your grandmother waiting for us in the canyon?"

John shrugged. "If we show up in twenty minutes or two hours, it won't make any difference to Grandmother. She expects us when she sees us. But we can go ahead and take the truck if you're in a hurry."

Victoria glanced across the dirt road at the dusty, blue Chevy pickup. A sudden vision of the brief, erotic fantasy she'd had the day before flashed through her mind. Passion-slicked skin and straining bodies tangled on the front seat. She looked away, glad she was wearing her sunglasses, and patted Scarlett's neck again. "I'd love to ride into the canyon." No way did she want to get into that truck with him. "Is Scarlett for hire?"

"Not on your life, tenderfoot." John waved a lazy arm toward the corral. "Pick any other horse you want, though."

"I'm not a tenderfoot," Victoria objected.

John raised an eyebrow, his glance running down her clinging, fashionably faded designer jeans to the pristine white leather tennis shoes on her feet.

"I didn't know I'd be doing any riding," she continued. "If I had, I'd've brought my boots."

"English riding boots, I suppose."

"Plain ol' standard-issue Western boots. Just like yours." She glanced down at his feet. "Only clean." And deep forest-green with fancy stitching around the tops, but he didn't have to know that.

"I work in my boots." John pushed himself away from the fence. "Well, come on, pick yourself a horse and let's get a move on." He looked up at her where she was perched on the top rail. "Or shall I pick one for you?"

"I prefer to choose my own mount, thank you." Nudging Scarlett out of the way as she spoke, Victoria pivoted around and swung one long leg over the top of the fence so that she was straddling it. One hand rested lightly on the rough-hewn rail between her splayed knees for balance. She tented the other over her sunglasses and scanned the horses.

John stood silently, hands on his hips in a characteristic pose, watching her look over the animals in the corral. He didn't think she really knew anything about horses—he figured someone else had probably chosen and paid for her Arabian—but it didn't matter. Any horse in the corral would do fine. From past experience with women like her, he figured she'd probably pick a mount because of color, or because it had soulful eyes or some other such thing. Silently he laid odds on Cottontop, a milk-white mare with a mane and tail like angel hair and all the spirit of a sleepy snail.

"That one," Victoria said finally. "The buckskin gelding."

John was impressed in spite of himself. The buckskin was second only to Scarlett. "Fine" was all he said, oddly disturbed to realize that she was a good judge of horseflesh. It didn't fit with the image he wanted to have of her. "Now let's see if you can saddle him by yourself."

"No problem," Victoria said, grasping the top rail with both hands as she prepared to climb down from the fence.

John watched her swing her leg out behind her, her sneakered foot dangling for a moment as she felt for the next rung. It took a conscious effort not to reach up to lift her down. She'd weigh no more than a feather, he thought. He already knew that her waist would be almost nothing in his hands. But touching her wasn't a good idea. It made him want to do more than just touch. Besides, she'd gotten up there without his help, he told himself sternly, forcing his eyes away from her enticing little derriere, she could get down the same way. Still, he moved a step closer, ready to catch her if she should fall.

"What's his name?" She jumped lightly to the ground, her hands still on the top rail as she stood facing the corral.

He was close enough to smell her perfume. "Whose?"

"The buckskin's."

Close enough so that he could lean forward and touch her hair with his cheek if he wanted to. And he wanted to. But he didn't. "Rover."

"Rover?" She turned her head slightly, looking over her shoulder as if she thought he might be pulling her leg. He was close. Too close. She whipped her head forward again, her hands tightening on the fence rail in front of her. "How did a horse get a name like Rover?"

she asked evenly, ignoring the sudden accelerated beating of her heart.

John stood where he was, inhaling the fragrance of her perfume, all the while telling himself to step back. *She's trouble*, his mind warned him. *But damned delicious trouble*, his body countered. "One of the kids thought he looked like an overgrown golden Lab," he said, his voice gruff.

Victoria continued to stare into the corral as if all her attention was focused on the oddly named horse. "Yes, I guess he does at that," she murmured coolly, every sense alive to the man standing so close behind her, waiting for what he would do next. It came as something of a shock to realize that what she wanted him to do was kiss her again.

"Well, hell," he breathed so low that she almost didn't hear the words. "Let's get a move on." He stepped back, away from temptation. "I've got better things to do than stand around all day admiring some damned fool horse."

SHE SAT A HORSE WELL—her spine ramrod straight, shoulders back, hips square, heels down, her erect posture displaying every mouth-watering curve of her slender body to advantage. Her rounded bottom shifted easily with every movement of the horse under her. Her unbound breasts bobbled and swayed with every lift and turn of her body as she twisted in the saddle, trying to take in all the sights at once. Her glossy hair, blacker and shinier than a raven's wing, brushed softly against her shoulders, lifting with every errant breeze that blew down the canyon.

It was driving him crazy.

So don't look, he told himself. But he couldn't help it. He seemed to have no willpower where Victoria Dillon was concerned.

Obviously his libido didn't care a whit that she wasn't an Indian woman, born and bred on the reservation, conversant with the Navajo way of life, committed to making that life better. It didn't care that she was obviously spoiled rotten and undoubtedly pampered right down to those glossy red nails, the kind of woman he'd vowed never to get involved with again—and never mind that she hadn't responded to him in any way that mattered. No. His libido didn't care about any of that. It only cared that she had the endless, elegant legs of a showgirl, the delicate bone structure of a fairy-tale princess and the eyes of a spitfire. Not that he could see her eyes through those outsize sunglasses she had on.

Thank God, he thought, shifting uneasily in the saddle.

What he could see was more than enough to set him fantasizing about what it would be like to see everything. All of her. Every inch of that warm, honey-colored skin bared to him. He'd like to snatch her off that horse and ride away with her somewhere, he decided, his eyes caressing the tanned skin of her bare arms. Back into the farthest reaches of the canyon, he thought, where he could lay her down in the cool shade of a peach tree and undress her slowly. He'd unbutton that pristine white blouse first, one button at a time, teasing them both with the slowness of it, and then—

"It's so beautiful here," Victoria said almost reverently, her voice breaking into his lascivious thoughts.

John pulled his hat lower and looked at Scarlett's ears.

"So cool and green and peaceful," she said. "Like a Garden of Eden in the middle of the desert." She reined in her horse, her eyes sweeping over the cottonwoods and peach trees and the sunflowers blooming in the small fields of corn that grew against the canyon walls.

A wide shallow stream, no more than a few inches deep in most places, flowed lazily along the middle of the canyon floor, providing a natural roadway for the residents. Sheer rock walls rose up to the sky on either side, long streaks of black and rust red, like paint that had been poured down from the rim, decorating almost every vertical surface. There was a faint scent of juniper in the air, and pine, and the fertile smell of the midday sun on growing things.

Victoria took a deep breath, her shoulders lifting in an appreciative sigh. It was so peaceful here in the canyon, in this corner of the world that civilization had rushed past and left dreaming of a time gone by. The perfect place to just sit and gather your thoughts and decide what to do with the rest of your life, she thought, wishing, for just a moment, that she could spend more time here than just the couple of days it would take to conclude her business.

"Lindsay's always said you had to see the Canyon de Chelly to believe it, but I never dreamed it would be like this," she said. "It's magnificent. The colors, the trees, the smell." Her arm swept out in a wide arc. "Everything. Pictures just don't do it justice." Saddle leather creaked as she twisted around to look at John. The excited smile of a child curved her glossy lips. "How soon do we get to one of those famous ruins?"

John couldn't help but respond to her eagerness with a smile of his own, despite the fact that his body was giving him no peace. "You'll see some just around that next bend up ahead there." He pressed his heels to Scarlett's sides. "Another five minutes at most if we—"

"Get a move on," Victoria finished for him, urging her own mount into motion as he came up even with her. They smiled at each other almost shyly. Their horses moved along side by side at a slow walk for a minute or two, both Victoria and John as silent as teenagers who had exchanged hellos and now didn't know what else to say.

For a while, back at the stable, she'd begun to think that maybe the feeling of tension between them was easing. They'd laughed together, amused by Scarlett's efforts to avoid the bit, and she'd seen a hint of grudging respect in his eyes when she'd saddled Rover with the ease of long practice. They'd even managed to exchange a glance or two that wasn't rife with speculation. But now it was back. The tension. The speculation. In both of them.

"Tell me about the ruins," she invited finally, unable to bear the silence a minute longer. "Who built them?"

John very nearly heaved a sigh of relief. He hadn't been able to think of anything to say either. "We call them the Anasazi. It means 'the ancient ones' in Navajo," he told her, calling easily on the stories he had heard repeated every summer of his life. "But no one really knows what they called themselves. According to archaeologists, **they** occupied the canyon for more than six hundred years and had quite an advanced culture. And then, somewhere around the fourteenth century, they disappeared."

"And no one knows why," she said, making it more a statement than a question. Victoria had heard some of the stories, too. Or at least read them. In her early teens, she had been briefly fascinated with all things Indian.

"And no one knows why," John agreed. "In any case, sometime in the mid-1700s the Navajo moved in. They lived pretty much then just as they do now. 'As the Navajo have always lived,' Grandmother would say."

"And that is?"

"Sheep herding and farming, mostly. Weaving and silversmithing and some basketry." He slanted her a lazy grin from under the brim of his hat. "With a little warring and raiding to keep things interesting."

Victoria pretended not to see that grin. "I've read that in the eighteen hun— Oh!" She pulled her mount up sharply as the first of the Anasazi ruins came into view. The crumbling remains of a culture long dead held her silent for a moment, awestruck that a people without cranes or bulldozers could build a whole village on the seemingly inaccessible ledges of the canyon walls. "It's magnificent, isn't it?" she said after a moment, still staring at the ruins. "And sad, too, in a way. I wonder what happened to them?"

"Drought seems the most likely answer. Tree-ring studies show that—"

"No, don't tell me." Victoria held up a hand to stop him. "I'd rather wonder."

"Do you want to get down and take a closer look?"

Victoria considered the idea for a moment. There were several people, tourists from the lodge, crawling over the lower level of the vaguely apartmentlike ruins, poking around into the past. It struck her as sacrilegious somehow. "No, I don't think so. I prefer to admire it from a distance."

"Well, come on then." He laid a rein against Scarlett's neck. "Let's—"

"Get a move on," Victoria said, unable to resist.

"That's two," he warned her. But he smiled as he said it.

"Tell me about the canyon," Victoria said as they guided the horses back into the center of the wide, shallow stream. "The canyon as it is today, I mean. You mentioned sheep herding and farming. What other crops grow in the canyon besides corn?"

"Squash and beans, mostly. Pumpkin." He gestured at a tree as they passed it. "Peaches." One of the big six-wheel sight-seeing vehicles lumbered into view, water splashing under its tires as it headed for the ruins that Victoria and John had just left. "Tourists," he said, lifting a hand to wave at the driver.

Some of the tourists—women mostly—waved back, thinking he was waving at them.

"Tourists are a crop?" Victoria asked when he turned his attention back to her.

"Probably the single biggest cash crop in the canyon. Without them there'd be no lodge, no sight-seeing trucks, no Indian guides. And there'd be far less market for Navajo handicrafts if the tourists stopped coming to the canyon. Or to the Navajo Nation in general, for that matter."

"You don't like having them here, do you?" she said, sensing something hidden beneath his easy words.

He shrugged, his wide shoulders straining the seams of his blue shirt. "It's not a question of liking or disliking. Tourists are necessary to the economy of the canyon. They're a fact of life," he said. "Just like the tourists who visit San Francisco or Paris every year."

"Well, I wouldn't like them here if this were my home."

John grinned at her tone of voice, like a queen banishing the peasants from her castle. *Spoiled little twit*, he thought again, but without the annoyance that had accompanied the thought before. "The canyon isn't exactly my home. Not in the way you mean."

"You don't live here?"

"Uh-uh. I visit."

"Visit?"

"Every summer since I was six years old."

"Is that when you were sent away to boarding school?" she asked, her tone hovering between disapproval and sympathy.

John's lips twitched at the hint of outrage in her voice. She'd obviously heard or read something about the injustices of the missionary and government boarding schools of fifty years ago. "No, that was when my parents got divorced and my mother moved us to Flagstaff."

"Flagstaff? You grew up in Flagstaff?" Victoria peered at him from behind her glasses. Divorced parents. Flagstaff. That explained something that had been nagging at her. He wasn't all Navajo. "Your mother isn't Indian," she said.

"Italian mostly. With a little Swiss mixed in somewhere."

"Ha! I knew it!" Victoria crowed. She twisted in the saddle to face him, inadvertently signaling Rover to stop. "No Indian alive ever had eyes like that."

He reined Scarlett in beside her. "Eyes like what?"

"Most Indians I've seen have brown eyes. Yours are kind of goldy green."

"Goldy green?" he repeated, startled. He hadn't thought she'd looked at him long enough to notice the color of his eyes. Or anything else, for that matter. "What kind of color is—?"

"John. Hey, John." A young Indian boy, about seven years old, hailed them from a stand of cottonwoods. "Hey, John-n-n-n!" he hollered, waving both arms above his head to make sure he had their attention.

"Hey, Ricky!" John hollered back. "What's up?"

"Grandmother sent me to look and see if you were comin' yet." He loped toward them, all bare brown arms and legs, his feet sending up sprays of water with every step. He grabbed John's stirrup when he was close enough, showing absolutely no fear of the big bay horse that side-stepped at his approach. "She said I could be the sentry. Christina, too," he added, speaking of his younger sister. "But I'm the *head* sentry. I sent her back to tell Grandmother you were coming as soon as I saw you."

"Head sentry, huh?" John reached down, grasped the child by the arm and hauled him up onto the saddle behind him. "That's a pretty important job."

"Yeah. Grandmother said she has better things to do than wait around all day."

A smile curved Victoria's lips. *"Twenty minutes or two hours,"* he'd said. *"It won't make any difference to Grandmother."* Evidently John didn't know his grandmother as well as he thought.

The child scrambled to his feet, balancing easily on the horse's rump, his arms around John's neck. "Where've you been, John?" he demanded, but he didn't wait for John's answer. "Grandmother said you probably got to sweet-talkin' some fool woman who should know better'n to trust a word you say, and forgot that you were supposed to bring the 'partment store lady," he said artlessly. "Were you?"

"Not unless he's got a pretty strange idea of sweet-talk," Victoria said under her breath.

John shot her a look. She returned it with a bland smile.

"Grandmother said to tell you she made tea for the 'partment store lady." He looked over at Victoria with the same shy, friendly smile she'd seen on other Navajo faces, and the bright, curious eyes of little boys everywhere. "You the 'partment store lady?"

Victoria's smile widened. "Yes, I am." She extended her hand. "My name's Victoria Dillon. What's yours?"

Ricky hesitated for just a moment. John nudged him. "I'm Ricky—Richard Redcloud," he said, his hand darting out to shake hers. He pulled it back as if he'd had a hold of a poisonous snake. "Grandmother's made some corn cakes for you, too," he told her, one arm still wrapped around John's neck. "With honey and pinyon nuts. But she won't let us have any till you get there."

"Then you'd better sit down so we can—" John began.

"Get a move on," Victoria finished for him.

"That's three," John said.

"Three!" Ricky shrieked in sudden excitement. "That's three!" Scarlett stirred restively, uneasy at the unfamiliar movement on her back. Ricky's arms merely tightened around John's neck. "You have to run," he told her.

"Run?" Victoria said.

"Ricky, sit down," John ordered, reaching behind him with one hand to pull the child down. He hauled the reins in tight with the other, holding Scarlett back.

Ricky slid to a sitting position. "But she has to run!"

"Why?" Victoria said.

"Because if you get three, he tickles you," Ricky said, exasperated that she didn't know the game.

"Tickles me?"

The smile John turned on her was wicked. "Until you beg for mercy," he said.

Victoria set her heels into Rover's sides and ran.

She heard the excited shriek of the child behind her, a muffled shout from John and then, a second later, the furious splashing of hoofs through water as he came after her. His horse was faster, she knew, but she had a slight head start, a second or two only, and he was handicapped by the child riding pillion. She leaned forward, urging her horse to more speed. "Come on, boy," she crooned, her voice as breathless and excited as Ricky's. "Come on."

The splashing behind her got louder.

She whooped wildly, the thrill of the chase tingling along her spine, the knowledge that her pursuer was John Redcloud adding a spice that was purely carnal.

"We're catching her, John!" Ricky shouted. "We're catching her!"

Victoria turned her head slightly at that, just enough to check his position. He was closing in on her, the bay's nose even with her horse's flank. She could see the flash of his teeth, bared in a warrior's grin.

"Come on, Rover. Come—"

One minute she was in the saddle, the next she was flying through the air. *What the hell*, she thought. And then she hit the ground, and everything went black.

5

THE FIRST THING Victoria became aware of as she drifted into consciousness was the strength of the arms holding her. The next thing was the inviting smell of the hard surface beneath her cheek. Part horse, part soap, all man. She turned her head slightly, burrowing into it.

"I think she's coming around."

The words rumbled under her ear, louder there than in the air above her head. She winced.

"Victoria?" A hand—hard, callused, gentle as a mother's on her newborn—touched her cheek. The words were equally gentle. "Victoria, can you hear me?"

She mumbled a denial and tried to burrow deeper into the smell, but the voice wouldn't leave her alone.

"Victoria?" The hand brushed wet strands of hair away from her face, cupped her cheek. "Come on, honey. I know you can hear me. Open your eyes like a good girl."

"No," she said quite clearly.

Another voice spoke then, a strangely mechanical flow of words issuing orders in a language that Victoria couldn't understand. She felt herself being lowered, felt something cool and clingy against her back as she was laid flat.

"Wet," she grumbled, frowning.

"Yes, you landed in the stream." The voice was farther away now. Not under her ear as it had been before. The strong arms, the comforting smell were gone. She stirred restively, wanting them back.

"Open your eyes, Victoria," the voice demanded again.

She struggled to obey. Her ebony lashes fluttered open, revealed nothing but a blur and drifted closed again, weighted by the clouds of unconsciousness that pressed her down. Something cold and damp wiped across her forehead, chasing them away. Another spate of incomprehensible words followed it, further prodding her into wakefulness. Victoria opened her eyes.

Above her, a face floated into focus. It was a face that had been carved by time. A woman's face, the years racing across it in random patterns over cheeks and chin and forehead, imprinting the copper-hued skin like the crazed surface of old and priceless pottery. Black eyes, bright, inquisitive, filled with the wisdom of the ages, stared down at her.

"Awake now?" the woman said in heavily accented English.

"Yes...yes, I'm awake. I think." Victoria lifted a hand to her head. She felt a bit light-headed and breathless, not quite headachy, but close. "What happened?"

"Your horse stumbled and threw you." The deep, musical voice came from somewhere outside her line of vision.

Victoria turned toward it. John. His Greek-god face wore a frown instead of a condescending smirk, and his eyes were serious. It was beginning to come back to her. They'd been racing down the middle of the stream.

She'd looked back—a stupid thing to do—and the next thing she knew she'd been flying through the air.

"Rover?" she said, struggling to sit up. "Is he all right?"

The old woman put a hand on Victoria's shoulder, holding her down. "Stay," she ordered.

Victoria subsided, too dizzy to make an issue of it right then. "Rover isn't hurt, is he?" she demanded of John, concern for her mount foremost in her mind.

"No, he isn't hurt," he soothed. "The question is, are you?"

"No, I don't think so. Just a bit light-headed." She levered herself up on one elbow. "I'll know better in a min—"

The old woman pushed her down again. "Stay," she ordered. A string of incomprehensible Navajo followed.

Victoria looked up at John for an interpretation.

"Grandmother says that you should lie still and let her make sure you haven't broken anything."

"I'm sure I haven't," Victoria began, but Maria Redcloud's weathered old hands were already running over her body, checking for breaks or bumps or strains. The expression on her equally weathered face brooked no argument. Victoria subsided and let her have her way.

The examination was over in a matter of minutes. "Okay," Maria said, nodding to herself. She sat back on her heels. "You stay," she ordered Victoria sternly, then turned to the three people ringed behind her. A quick instruction sent the wide-eyed little girl racing toward the six-sided log structure across the clearing.

Another had John and Ricky backing out of the open shelter where Victoria lay.

Again, Victoria's eyes sought John's.

"Grandmother wants to get you out of those wet clothes," he said. A grin flickered across his handsome face. "And she doesn't want Ricky and me to watch."

"I don't need to change," Victoria argued. "In this heat my clothes will dry in no time." She looked toward the old woman. "Really, Mrs. Redcloud," she said, managing to sit up. Her head throbbed with the movement, but she ignored it. "All I need to do is sit out in the sun for a while."

Maria Redcloud spoke to her grandson again, reaching out to take the garments that her great-granddaughter brought to her.

"English, Grandmother," John began, but Maria cut him off with a shake of her head and a quick impatient tumble of words.

John shrugged. "All right," he replied, agreeing with whatever she had said to him. He looked back at Victoria. "Grandmother says to tell you not to be so difficult and stubborn and to do as she says. After you've changed into something dry, you can have a cup of tea. If that stays down you can have a corn cake. But you're to stay right there in the shade and rest until she says you can get up."

"But I feel fine," Victoria lied. "Really."

Maria shook her head forcefully, as if she had understood what Victoria said, and waved her menfolk away from the open-air structure.

"John, tell her," Victoria said as Maria reached for the buttons on her blouse. "I don't need to change."

John shrugged, grinning at her predicament. "Won't do any good," he said. "Grandmother's as stubborn as they come. I'll be glad to stay and try to convince her, though," he offered, his eyes dropping to where Maria's busy fingers had slipped the third button of Victoria's wet blouse.

Victoria gasped, realizing that the blouse was plastered to her front. She wasn't wearing anything underneath it. "Get out of here," she said, reaching up to keep Maria from baring her breasts in front of the grinning idiot who was her grandson.

"Come on, Ricky. Let's go see if we can round up the horses," John said, turning away as Maria lifted one of the dry garments from her lap.

With a deft maneuver that would have done credit to a professional dresser, she dropped a faded red calico tunic over Victoria's head, then reached under and pulled the white blouse off her shoulders beneath it. Peeling it down her patient's arms, she handed the damp garment to the waiting child to drape across the branches of a nearby bush. Victoria slipped her arms into the sleeves of the borrowed blouse with hardly an inch of bare skin having been exposed.

After divesting her of her wet sneakers, Maria stood and helped Victoria to her feet. The calico tunic fell almost to midthigh. With hand gestures and facial expressions, the old woman made it clear that she wanted Victoria to take off her jeans, too. She complied, pushing the damp jeans down her legs, then stepping into the wide cotton skirt that Maria held for her. Feeling a bit shaky, she started to sink back down.

"All," Maria said, motioning toward her hips.

"What?"

"All," Maria repeated, and then said something in Navajo.

"I don't..." Victoria looked toward the little girl. "Do you speak English?"

"Grandmother wants you to take off what's under," the child said. "To dry." She motioned to where the white blouse and jeans were spread out in the sun.

"Oh, well...all right," Victoria said, willing to do whatever would allow her to sit back down the fastest. She felt a little woozy. Not dizzy exactly, but unstable enough that she didn't want to be on her feet for too long right now. She flicked up the sides of the skirt, hooked her thumbs in the sides of the underpants and slid them down her legs. "Here."

The child took the tiny scrap of lace and hung it up to dry with the rest of the clothes.

"Thank you...Christina, isn't it?" Victoria said, sinking back down on the sheepskins she'd been lying on a few moments before. She felt much better sitting down.

The child beamed. "Yes, I am Christina," she said shyly.

"Well, thank you, Christina, you've been a big help."

The child stood there, smiling at her until Maria issued a command that sent her running off in the direction John and her brother had taken a few minutes before.

Victoria wriggled around a bit then, settling herself on the sheepskins, her gaze taking in the scene before her. It was as if a picture in a history book had suddenly come to life; the open-sided structure made of four upright poles and a leafy, latticed top that sheltered her from the sun, the sheepskin rugs piled under her, the upright loom that stood less than an arm's length away, the six-sided hogan across the small clearing, the old Indian woman leaning over the camp stove that was set up just outside the shelter. Mostly the old woman.

Victoria leaned back against the sheepskins and watched Maria Redcloud from under lowered lashes, fascinated by this living glimpse of the past.

She was attired in the same sort of clothing that Navajo women had worn since the early 1860s. A deep green velveteen tunic, long-sleeved and high-collared, was tucked into a full, ankle-length calico skirt. A lavish silver-and-turquoise-embellished concha belt cinched her waist. A many-stranded necklace of turquoise beads hung around her neck, along with a delicately wrought silver-and-turquoise cross. More fine examples of the silversmith's art adorned her wrists. Her heavy gray hair was smoothed back into a traditional wrapped knot at the back of her head. And on her feet were—

Victoria blinked, then looked again, making sure she had seen what she thought she had. Yes, on her feet Maria Redcloud wore black Converse high-tops. It was startling and incongruous, that bit of mainstream America on the feet of a living relic of the past, but somehow appropriate. The Navajo had always been known for adapting the ways of other cultures to the needs of their own, choosing those aspects of it that suited them and leaving the rest. Maria Redcloud had apparently found high-top sneakers suited to her needs.

"Take," Maria said then, thrusting an enameled tin cup under Victoria's nose.

Victoria sat up straight and took it. The scent of some kind of herbal tea wafted up to tickle her nose. "Thank you." She took a cautious sip of the contents. Hot but not too hot. Strong but not too strong. Liquid comfort. "Thank you," she said again, a wide smile conveying her appreciation nonverbally. "It's just what I needed."

Maria nodded curtly and turned away, picking up a long-handled spoon to stir the pot of stew that simmered on the camp stove.

Victoria leaned back against the sheepskins behind her and sipped at the tea, mentally running a hand over her body, asking herself how she felt. She must have just had the wind knocked out of her when she fell, she decided after a moment. Certainly nothing more serious than that. The woozy feeling was already fading. The tea was staying down with no problem. The smell from the camp stove was reminding her that she hadn't had breakfast.

"The horses are all taken care of, Grandmother," Ricky said, as he came running up to the shelter ahead of John, who carried Christina on his shoulders. "Can we have our corn cakes now?"

In answer, Maria opened a covered basket decorated with a black geometric design and took out what looked to Victoria like two large, thick sugar cookies. She handed them to Ricky with a few quick words of instruction.

"Aw, Grandmother—" Ricky began, his dark eyes sliding toward Victoria.

"Don't argue, Ricky," John admonished, reaching up to grasp Christina by the forearms. He lifted her over his head and lowered her to the ground. "Grandmother wants to talk to her guest alone. So give Christina her corn cake and take off."

Ricky stood there for a moment, looking as if he would like to argue the point. While he vacillated, Christina reached out and deftly plucked her cake from her brother's hand.

"There was a load of tourists just pulled up to the White House Ruins when we rode by," John said. "Maybe one of them will give you a quarter to pose for them."

Both children squealed and scampered off, Ricky in the lead as usual. John stood watching, a fond smile on his face, until they disappeared through the trees. Then he turned and strolled into the shade of the shelter. He crouched in front of Victoria.

"How're you feeling?" he said softly.

"Fine."

"No headache?"

"No."

"Blurred vision?"

She shook her head.

"Dizziness?"

"A little at first but only for a minute. And it's gone now," she said, looking at him over the rim of her cup. The sunlight filtered through the leafy branches overhead, casting patterns of dark and light across his face and hair. His eyes, more green than gold in the dappled light, were concerned and friendly, with no trace of the arrogant male who was so good at getting her back up.

Not that he didn't look as deliciously Greek-god hunky crouched there in front of her, his elbows balanced on his splayed knees, as he did towering over her with that macho grin on his face. But this way, in this mood, he seemed much more approachable, she decided. A man she could like as well as drool over. She smiled.

"You gave us quite a scare," he said, wondering just want the hell she was smiling at like that, all sort of soft and secret and pleased with herself.

"Did I?"

"You did." He reached out and tucked a strand of hair behind her ear. Even wet, it was as soft as silk. He resisted the urge to smooth it with his palm. "You collapsed like a rag doll when you hit the ground."

Victoria felt a bit like a rag doll at the moment, boneless and pliant. And just a little drowsy. She wasn't sure whether it was John or the heat or the fact that she'd recently taken a nosedive off the back of a galloping horse. But it didn't matter. "How long was I out?"

"A minute, maybe."

"That's all?"

His mouth quirked up at the corner. "Isn't that enough?"

She shrugged, her fingers playing along the edge of the tin cup, her eyes never leaving his. "It seemed longer."

"Take it from me, it was plenty long enough. The way you hung there when I picked you up, Ricky was sure you were dead."

"Well, I'm just fine now." She gestured languidly toward the clothes she wore. "Dry." She glanced over to where Maria was still occupied at the stove, then leaned forward. "And hungry," she whispered. "I want that corn cake you promised me."

John laughed, delighted. He had been halfway expecting her to be annoyed by the whole situation; upset by the fact that the clothes she was wearing were old and unfashionable; irritated because her hair was hanging damp and tangled around her face and no one had offered her a comb. But she just sat there, smiling at him over her cup, obviously enjoying what she could have easily turned into an unpleasant experience for all of them. Maybe she wasn't quite as spoiled as he'd first thought.

"If you're not going to get me a corn cake," she said, her lower lip thrust out in the suggestion of a pout, "may I have some more tea?" She held out her empty cup, clearly expecting him to get up and refill it for her.

And then again, he thought, *maybe she is*. Somehow it didn't bother him as much as it had before. He took her cup and rose to his feet.

"Any more tea, Grandmother?"

Maria nodded and took the cup. "Just half," she said to him in Navajo.

"Only half?" John asked also in that language. "What's in it?"

Maria shrugged. "Just a few herbs. To soothe her in case she has a headache after her fall. Too much will make her sleepy."

John looked over at Victoria. She gave him the sweet, dreamy smile of a tired child. He smiled back. "I think she's already had too much."

"Yes?" Maria hurried over to check her patient. She knelt down, placing a gnarled hand under Victoria's chin. "Look," she said in English, touching a finger to the corner of her own eye. Victoria stared at her with the studied concentration of a baby owl. Maria placed a hand over her eyes for a moment, then took it away. Her pupils reacted normally. "She is fine," Maria said in her own language.

Victoria yawned. "Oh, I'm sorry." She lifted a hand to cover her mouth. "That was very rude of me." Her eyes sought John's. "Tell her I'm sorry," she said as Maria straightened. "I didn't mean to yawn in her face like that. I don't know what came over me."

"The tea."

"What?"

"The tea," John repeated. "It has a mild sedative in it."

"Oh." Victoria stifled another yawn. "Well, I'm sorry, anyway. Please tell her for me."

"She knows," John assured her. "Grandmother understands English *quite* well," he added, slanting a wry glance at the old woman.

Maria ignored him and went back to her stove.

John crouched in front of Victoria again. "Why don't you put your head down and take a little nap," he suggested, reaching out to nudge her back against the sheepskins.

"What about my corn cake?"

"I'll save one for you." He nudged her again, pulling her supporting elbow out from under her so that she lay flat. "You can have it when you wake up. Okay?"

"Okay." Victoria smiled up at him sleepily, her hair spread out on the sheepskins, her eyes half closed, her mouth soft, her body lax. Like a woman waiting to be loved.

John felt something tighten inside him. Desire, he told himself, denying that it might be anything more dangerous—like tenderness. She wasn't a woman he wanted to feel tenderness for. He couldn't afford to feel *anything* for a woman like her. It didn't fit in with his life's plans. "Close your eyes and go to sleep, Victoria," he said softly.

Her eyes closed, the lashes fluttering down like black lace fans over her elegant cheekbones. She sighed and curled to her side, lifting her hands to tuck them beneath her cheek. John reached out and gently, tenderly smoothed her ebony hair away.

Maria watched him with a frown on her face. "Who is she?" she demanded, handing him a cup of tea—sans sedative—when he rose to his feet.

John's fingers curled around the enameled cup. "Who's who?" he began, then added, "Oh, I forgot you didn't know. Her name is Victoria Dillon." He took a sip of his tea. "Sister-in-law of the woman you were expecting."

"What happened to the other one?"

"She's going to have a baby. Babies," he corrected himself, settling down on a conveniently placed rock so that his back was warmed by the sun, his face shaded by the leafy branches overhead. Victoria was in his direct line of vision. "Her husband didn't want her driving all over Arizona by herself."

"And so they sent this one." Maria gestured toward the sleeping woman with her spoon. "Does she know anything about Navajo weaving or basketry?"

"I assume so," John answered absently, staring at Victoria's bare feet. They were small and narrow, the rounded bones of her ankles as fragile as a bird's. Her glossy red toenails looked exotic against the faded cotton skirt and sheepskin rugs. "It wouldn't make much sense for her to be here if she didn't."

A disgruntled snort was Maria's only reply to that. "Does she have a husband?"

"I don't know." He denied the quick surge of emotion that welled up in him at the suggestion that she might be married. "I didn't ask her."

"But you look at her."

He raised his eyes to his grandmother's. "She's a beautiful woman," he defended himself mildly. "I like looking at beautiful women."

"She is a white-eyes." There was no hate in the words, no anger, just a warning.

John sighed and swirled the tea in his cup. "I know that, Grandmother." He'd reminded himself of it often enough in the past thirty-six hours—every time he'd looked at her and been tempted.

She was an Anglo. Non-Indian. More, she was a city woman. There was nothing intrinsically wrong with any of those things. They were fine in their place. But their place was not here in the Canyon de Chelly, nor anywhere in the Navajo Nation. Not on any permanent sort of basis. If, in his thirty-three years, his mother hadn't been able to teach him that, his ex-wife certainly had. With a vengeance. After the divorce, he'd promised himself that when he got involved again, *if* he got involved again, it would be with a Navajo woman who would understand his way of life and his loyalties.

There was no place in his life for another city woman, especially not one who'd probably learned to give orders to the maid about the same time she'd learned to talk.

Not that there was a snowball's chance in hell of anything developing, anyway, he told himself, watching her nestle deeper into the sheepskins. She'd be gone in a few days; surely he could leave her alone for that long.

"You look at her still," Maria said accusingly.

John didn't deny it. He didn't take his eyes off of her, either. "And that's all I'm going to do, Grandmother. Just look. No harm in looking, is there?"

6

VICTORIA AWOKE TO the muted music of the breeze rustling through the leafy roof above her head and a soft, rhythmic, scraping sound that she couldn't quite place. She continued to lie with her eyes closed for a minute or two, listening to the peaceful sounds and luxuriating in the warmth and softness all around her. She felt deliciously, completely rested for the first time in months, contented as a cat curled up in the sun. She stretched lazily and opened her eyes, turning her head to locate the source of the scraping sound.

It was Christina. She sat cross-legged in a corner of the shelter, head bent, her whole attention focused on the fluffy bundle in her lap. Victoria propped herself up on an elbow, fascinated to realize that the child was carding wool. Scraping together two wide, wooden-backed brushes shaped like curry combs, she cleaned and disentangled the wool, preparing it to be spun. Victoria had seen pictures of the process but had never seen it done. And the child did it so competently, so easily, as if she had been doing it all her short life.

"Hello," Victoria said softly, not wanting to startle the little girl.

Christina looked up. A friendly smile curved her lips. "Oh, you're awake." She put the cards and wool aside and jumped to her feet. "I'll go get Grandmother."

"No, that's all right," said Victoria, pushing herself to a sitting position. "Don't interrupt your work."

"It's okay. Grandmother told me to get her as soon as you woke up." Christina dashed off.

Victoria stretched again, linking her hands above her head and arching her back. She felt so good, so...euphoric almost, silly as that sounded. She didn't even have a twinge of the aches that should have been the reward for her carelessness on Rover. She looked around the silent shelter as she lowered her arms, wondering how long she'd been asleep. Wondering, too, where John was.

John.

She'd dreamed about him, she remembered suddenly, the images of their entwined bodies rushing to fill her waking mind. Scandalous dreams. Dreams that made her fantasy of heated, frantic lovemaking in the cab of his truck pale by comparison. He'd been tender as well as passionate in her dreams, loving as well as lustful. He'd touched her with those hard, callused hands of his in ways that she never even knew she wanted to be touched. He'd looked at her with a desperate need in those hot amber eyes. Spoken her name on a breathy sigh. Heat coiled through her body as the images replayed in her mind. Ruthlessly she pushed them aside. It was troubling and . . . and disconcerting, she thought, for want of a better word. Yes, definitely disconcerting to dream such dreams about a man she'd only met yesterday afternoon. A man who wasn't even her type—despite his impressive physical attributes.

And she was glad he wasn't here now, she told herself, blood rushing to her cheeks at the mere *thought* of facing him with those dreams fresh in her mind. But still—

Had he really left her here, all alone, at the mercy of his grandmother?

It seemed he had, for there was Maria, walking toward the shelter, with only Christina in attendance.

"Better?" Maria asked, stepping into the shade.

"Yes. I'm fine." Victoria glanced down, carefully straightening the hem of her skirt as she spoke. She wouldn't be at all surprised to find that Maria Redcloud was some sort of Navajo shaman who could divine her dreams with a glance.

"I look," Maria said, obviously not trusting her patient's judgment. She bent over, grasping Victoria's chin with one hand as she had before, and covered her eyes with the other. Her hands were small and strong, with a ridge of calluses along the tips of her fingers and a blend of gentleness and firmness in her touch that spoke of a woman who'd handled generations of children. She took her hand away and peered into Victoria's eyes as if she were trying to see into her soul. Victoria tried to look innocent. "Okay," Maria said, releasing her chin. "Hungry now?"

Victoria let out a breath she didn't know she'd been holding. "Yes, I am. Ravenous," she said, meaning it. The stew simmering on the camp stove was making her mouth water. Was it possible, she wondered, for imaginary sex to work up an appetite? "But I'd like to use the bathroom first," she said, glancing hopefully toward the six-sided hogan. Was there such a thing as indoor plumbing in the Canyon de Chelly?

Maria gestured to Christina.

"I'll show you where it is," the child said, reaching for Victoria's hand as she came to her feet. They started down a well-worn path, one that led away from the family's living quarters. So much for indoor plumbing, Victoria thought, adjusting her expectations downward. If the bathroom turned out to be anything more than a stop behind the nearest bush, she'd count herself lucky.

She'd be lucky, too, if she didn't break her neck stumbling over the edge of the too-long skirt she wore. She gathered the excess material in her free hand, head down as she carefully picked her way along the path. Christina, she thought, must have rawhide on the bottoms of her little brown feet; she didn't seem to feel the rocks at all.

"There," the child said then, pointing toward a small outhouse, complete with a half-moon carved high in the door.

Victoria entered it cautiously. The inside was scrupulously clean, stiflingly hot and smelled strongly of disinfectant and lye. The chemical toilet had a flush mechanism. Victoria used it quickly and returned to the fresh air outside.

"You can wash here," said Christina, motioning toward a large earthenware jug suspended from a metal bracket on the outhouse. A wide shallow bowl sat on a wooden shelf beneath it, a bar of soap in a dish beside it. Christina waited until Victoria held her hands under the jug before turning the butterfly clip on the spigot. Sun-warmed water flowed out. Victoria washed her hands, shook off the excess water, then dried them on her skirt.

"All finished?" the child asked, dumping the used water on the ground.

"Yes. Thank you, Christina."

"You're welcome." She set the bowl back on the shelf and reached for Victoria's hand with the air of an adult about to lead a child across a busy street. Obviously she was under orders to let her charge come to no harm.

"Wait a minute," Victoria said, hanging back when Christina would have started up the path.

The child cast a dubious look upward. Delays were not on her agenda.

"My skirt's too long," Victoria explained, bending down to lift the hem. Giving it a couple of twists to gather in the material, she tucked it into the waistband of her skirt. It formed an ungainly lump under the calico tunic. "Not exactly haute couture, hmm?"

Christina smiled at her, understanding the meaning if not the words.

"Well, who cares?" Victoria held her hand out. "Lead me back to the patio."

"Patio?" Christina said, her sweet little face screwed up in a frown.

"The place where we were." Victoria lifted her free hand, waving it around over her head. "With the leafy top."

"The *ramada*," Christina supplied.

"The *ramada*," Victoria repeated dutifully. She had always thought a *ramada* was where you kept horses. Or was that a *ramuda*?

Christina walked silently beside her.

Navajo children, Victoria reflected, staring down at the neat part in Christina's dark brown hair, chattered much less than their Anglo counterparts. Or perhaps they were just shyer with strangers. Especially Anglo strangers.

She wondered what to say to draw her out. Victoria wasn't usually at a loss for conversation, but then she didn't usually converse with wide-eyed Indian children. For a moment, she considered asking her a few questions about John. A sure-fire conversation starter, perhaps, but it smacked of pumping the child for information.

Besides, Victoria reminded herself, she wasn't going to think of John Redcloud anymore. She would be leaving as soon as her business was completed and would never see him again. There was no future in thinking about him. She didn't even *want* to think about him.

Oh, he was gorgeous, sure, and he possessed a certain natural charm that might overwhelm a less-sophisticated woman, but he was far too arrogant and chauvinistic ever to appeal to her on any more than a physical level. And she looked for more than just the physical in a man, in a relationship. So there was absolutely no reason why she should want to know any more about him than she already did. And she didn't, she told herself. She really didn't.

"How old are you, Christina?" she asked, deliberately tearing her mind away from thoughts of John Redcloud. "About seven?"

"I am six." Christina smiled, pleased to have been taken for older.

"And you already know how to card wool. You must be pretty smart."

Christina's smile grew wider. "All little girls know how to card wool," she said truthfully. "But Grandmother says I will be as good a weaver as she is when I grow up," the child added proudly. "When I am twelve, or maybe sooner, she will help me build my own loom."

"You'll have to let me know when that happens," Victoria said, watching the path for stones. "I want to buy your rugs for our store."

"Really?" Christina paused to stare up at the woman beside her, excitement shining in her eyes. "You will buy my rugs, just like Grandmother's?"

"Really," Victoria responded with a nod. Navajo children, she decided then, were very much like other children, after all. You just had to find out what interested them. "You don't think I'd want anyone else to get your rugs, do you?"

"Wait until I tell Ricky," she said gleefully, pulling on Victoria's hand in an effort to hurry her along. "He thinks girls can't do *anything*."

"I wonder where he got that idea?" Victoria mumbled, hot-footing it along the path as she tried to keep up with Christina and avoid stepping on any rocks at the same time.

That was how John saw her—being dragged up the path from the outhouse by the excited, bright-eyed child, her raven hair in a bewitching tangle, her skirt tucked up around the most tantalizing pair of legs he'd ever seen, her bare feet dusty. At first glance, she could have been mistaken for an Indian herself, if a slightly untidy one. Her coloring was right—the smooth honey-gold skin, the black hair and dark chocolate eyes. Even the cheekbones, high and sharp, were right. One of the tourists from the lodge, catching a glimpse of her through the trees, wouldn't even be aware that he was seeing an illusion.

But a second, closer glance revealed her for what she was. The smooth, professionally cared for hands, the gleaming red toenails, the aristocratic elegance and air of pampered wealth all said she was accustomed to silks and satins and gauzy, billowing linens, no matter how casually she wore faded calico. One good look at her would tell the careful observer that she was a woman unaccustomed to hard work, unacquainted with personal sacrifice. In a word, she was spoiled. Used to being done for, rather than doing. And she most certainly wasn't for him.

He didn't even want her, anyway, John told himself, not in any way that really mattered. But, Lord, he'd love to have her in all the ways that didn't!

He'd sat there, watching her while she slept, and *ached* to lie down beside her. If they'd been alone, he might have done just that. She'd have been warm and receptive in his arms, returning his kisses before she even came fully awake. And then, when she was soft and sighing and ready for him, he'd have run his hand up her bare leg, up under that wide cotton skirt and—

"Ricky! Ricky!" Christina called then, catching sight of her brother in the shade of the *ramada*. "Guess what! I'm going to have my rugs in a store!" She released Victoria's hand to run up the path ahead of her.

John pulled himself up sharply. Fantasizing again, he thought, disgusted. He'd been doing entirely too much of that lately—ever since the moment he'd pulled up behind that flashy little Mercedes. He vowed to stop it.

As soon as she left, maybe, and he didn't have to look at her and wonder how she would feel lying under him.

"You look fully recovered," he said, stepping out into the sun. "No residual effects?"

Victoria resisted the urge to yank her skirt down. "I'm fine, thank you," she said, willing herself not to lift her hands to smooth her hair. She just knew it was a rat's nest of tangles.

Not that she cared, of course, except for what Maria Redcloud would think of her. It was unprofessional for a department-store buyer to call on a supplier looking as if she hadn't been near a mirror in weeks. She was sure that Lindsay never had. But why worry about being unprofessional now? Arriving wet and unconscious, dangling like a rag doll in the arms of the supplier's grandson because she hadn't been smart enough to stay on her horse, had to be the height of unprofessionalism. Nothing to do but brazen it out. Victoria lifted her chin.

"I'm glad you're back," she said to John as she walked past him into the shade of the *ramada*. "I need someone to interpret."

"Interpret?" John inquired, his hackles rising instantly at the way she spoke to him. As if he were a servant in her house, an employee who wouldn't even consider saying no to her.

"For your grandmother and me," she told him, not even turning around to see if he followed her. "Mrs. Redcloud," she said, coming up behind the woman where she bent over the camp stove. "I'd like to thank you for your kindness and understanding and find out when we might discuss our business. I—"

Her words were cut off as Maria turned and thrust an enameled plateful of lamb stew into her hands. "Eat first," she said.

"It looks delicious," Victoria began, standing there with the plate in her hands. The smell was mouth-watering. "But I've taken up so much of your time already today and—"

"Eat first," Maria repeated, filling another plate for her grandson.

"But, Mrs. Redcloud, I really—"

"Eat first," Maria said firmly. "Talk after."

"Need me to interpret that for you?" John asked, taking the plate from his grandmother.

Victoria ignored him. *Smart ass*, she thought as he sauntered over to where Ricky and Christina were already sitting cross-legged, eagerly sopping up the rich gravy with folded pieces of corn tortillas. Plate in hand, he dropped down across from the children.

Victoria tried again. "Mrs. Redcloud," she began, clutching the plate. "Perhaps we could discuss the sale of your rugs while we—"

Maria straightened from the stove, her own plate of food in her hands. "No talk now. Eat," she said, moving past Victoria to join the circle of her family.

Victoria sighed and followed her hostess. John watched her with a smirk on his face, waiting for her to attempt the cross-legged position with a full plate in her hand and the wide skirt fluttering around her legs. She made it look easy, sinking gracefully to the ground between Maria and Christina. The skirt puffed out around her. It covered her right leg completely, but the other leg, on the side where her skirt was tucked into the waistband, was bare nearly to the top of her thigh.

Luscious thigh, he thought, scooping up a bite of stew with a tortilla. Pretty rounded knee. Sleek, well-toned calf. Definitely a world-class leg. A feast of firm, tantalizing female flesh. Mouth-watering.

He'd like to nibble on that leg sometime, starting at that elegant ankle and working slowly upward. And then, when he reached the top of her thigh, he'd nuzzle her skirt aside and drive them both crazy. He knew she wasn't wearing anything under it. He'd seen that little white scrap of material she probably called panties drying in the sun with the rest of her clothes. His glance flickered over to the bush where it hung. Nothing but a bit a lace held together with strips of ribbon. He wondered why she bothered wearing it at all. He looked back toward the smooth bare expanse of her thigh.

She had pulled the skirt down over her knee.

He looked up into her face. Their eyes locked. Hot amber burned into bubbling bittersweet chocolate, a tangle of warring emotions sizzling between them. Speculation. Desire. Denial. They both looked away, down into their plates. Victoria could feel herself flushing, the heat rising up to stain her cheeks. She had to resist the urge to straighten her legs and press her thighs together. John shifted where he sat, cursing the hot blood that climbed up the back of his neck. He lowered his plate to his lap, hiding the bulge that pressed against the fly of his jeans.

"I have decided that I must know this Victoria Dillon better," Maria said in Navajo, the words slicing through the emotions that simmered between them.

Recognizing her name, Victoria glanced toward her hostess expectantly.

John continued staring at his plate. "Know her better how?" he said. Irritably he pushed his stew around with the tortilla, the motion jerky.

"I must know her soul before I can entrust her with my rugs."

John's head snapped up. The tortilla stilled in his hand. "You must know her what?"

"Her soul," Maria repeated serenely.

"What?" Victoria said. "What did she say?"

John ignored her. "Her soul? What in blazes for?" He eyed his grandmother suspiciously. "What are you up to, Grandmother?"

"I am up to nothing," Maria said with a dignified sniff. "I merely wish to know what sort of a woman she is before I entrust her with my rugs and those of the other women of our clan."

"Why? You never wanted to know her sister-in-law's soul."

"I could see what kind of woman the other one was at a glance." She looked over at Victoria. "I cannot see this one so clearly."

"What's she saying?" Victoria repeated. She could tell that the conversation was about her, even if she couldn't understand a word being said. She could also tell that John didn't like whatever his grandmother was saying.

John waved her to silence. "Why do you need to see her clearly? What difference does it make?"

"I must know if she will treat my rugs with the reverence they require."

"Reverence?" His grandmother was up to something. He didn't know what or why, but she was definitely up to something. *Reverence, my ass*, he thought. Maria Redcloud didn't give a tinker's damn whether Victoria would treat her rugs with reverence. As long as she paid a good price for them, that was all that mattered. John set his plate down. "What exactly do you mean, Grandmother?"

"I mean only what I say, Grandson."

Victoria looked toward the two children, silent and wide-eyed as they listened to their grandmother and John exchange words. "What are they saying?"

Maria spoke before either of them could answer. "Have you finished eating?" she said to them in Navajo.

The children nodded.

"Then you may each have another corn cake before you go," she said, motioning toward the covered basket that held the treats. "The garden needs weeding."

Without another word the children rose to their feet, got their corn cakes and headed toward the family garden.

"What's going on?" Victoria said again, demand edging her voice. She knew without being told that they were talking about her. She wanted to know what was being said. And she wanted to know now. "What's she saying, John?"

"Grandmother wants to know your soul."

"My soul?" Her glance flickered back and forth between the two of them. There was something going on here, some undercurrent that she didn't understand. "What about my soul?"

"Exactly what I want to know," said John. He gave Maria a pointed look. "Grandmother?"

Maria spread her gnarled hands. "It is as I have said. I wish to know this young woman before I sell my rugs to her. I wish to know what kind of person she is—" she touched a hand to her chest "—inside."

"John?" Victoria said, her eyes asking for an interpretation.

John told her what his grandmother had said.

She frowned, not understanding. Lindsay had never mentioned anything about this. She had simply gone to the canyon, bargained for the rugs and come home. What did the kind of person she was have to do with the purchase of Maria Redcloud's rugs?

"Please tell her I don't understand. What exactly does she want to know? I'll be happy to tell her what I can, of course, but..." She shrugged. "I'm not sure what she wants from me," she finished, her eyes on Maria's lined face as if she might see the answer there.

"Grandmother?" John said.

"Tell her I wish to know nothing specifically. But I would like her to stay in the canyon—" she moved her arm in a graceful arc, taking in the *ramada*, the clearing, the hogan "—here, as my guest, for a day or two so that I may know her."

"A day or two?" John's eyes narrowed. He'd be tied in knots of frustration if Victoria Dillon stayed with them for a day or two. "Why?"

Maria ignored her grandson's question. "Or perhaps a week."

"A week!" John said in English. A week of looking at Victoria Dillon would turn him into a raving maniac.

"A week?" Victoria echoed, looking back and forth between them. "A week what?"

But they didn't even glance at her.

"I cannot tell exactly how long it will take." Maria shrugged, unaffected by her grandson's irritation.

"How long *what* will take?" he demanded.

"Knowing her soul," she repeated patiently.

"You couldn't care less about the state of her soul," John said, thoroughly exasperated now. "What's the real reason?"

"I have told you my reason," Maria said stubbornly.

"Grandmother . . ." He passed a hand down his face. "Dammit," he swore, frustrated. "What's gotten into you? Not two hours ago you were warning me against just looking at her!"

Maria nodded toward their guest. "Tell her what I have said."

John sighed. When Maria got that look on her face there was no reasoning with her. He knew—he'd tried. All it had ever gotten him was hoarse. He would just have to accept that, for some reason of her own, his grandmother wanted Victoria to stay for a few days. He didn't know why; he couldn't even begin to guess what she hoped to accomplish by it, but logically, what harm could it do? Besides driving him into an acute state of sexual frenzy. "Grandmother says she wants to know what kind of person you are," he said to Victoria.

"Yes, I understand that part, but—"

"She wants you to stay here for a few days while she gets to know you."

"Stay...?" Victoria did some quick mental calculations. A few days wouldn't really matter one way or the other. She wasn't on a schedule, and she was stuck here, anyway, until her car was fixed. Two or three days the mechanic had said. And the canyon was a beautiful place; she'd thought so immediately. A few extra days of enjoying its peacefulness and beauty would be no hardship at all. "I guess I could extend my reservations at the lodge," she said hesitantly. "I'd have to call home and let them know I'm staying on, but—"

"Not at the lodge," John said. "Here."

"Here?" Her eyes widened. "You mean right here? In the canyon?" That put a whole different slant on things. Staying at the lodge where she might run into John when she came out to visit Maria was one thing. Staying in his home was something else entirely. "With you?"

"Grandmother?" John said, hoping she'd see how impossible the situation was.

Maria nodded her head. "Here," she said in English.

"But I... That is—" She couldn't stay in the hogan with Maria and John and the children and who knew who else! Especially not with John. Ignoring him and his gorgeous body would be impossible in the confines of the Redcloud hogan. "Wouldn't it be kind of crowded?" she asked finally.

"Damned crowded," agreed John. He didn't live in Maria's hogan as Victoria obviously thought. He had a small one of his own just through the trees that he used whenever he stayed overnight in the canyon. But it would still be too damned crowded.

"Well, then . . . ?"

"You see the problem, Grandmother?" he said in English. Victoria was too wrapped up in imagining how it would be to sleep in the same room as John—*with* John—to realize that Maria hadn't needed a translation to understand them.

"She can have a tent of her own. From the lodge. You can put it up for her," she said in Navajo. She cast an assessing look at Victoria, who looked back blankly, not understanding a word that was being said. "I do not think she can do it for herself."

"No," John agreed in English. "I doubt she can."

"Doubt I can what?"

"Put up a tent."

"A tent? What tent? Why?" Frustration at having to ask what was being said made her voice sharp. Her own rioting imagination made her . . . tense.

"Grandmother suggests that you should have your own tent during your visit. The lodge rents them out to a limited number of campers." He paused. "Or I could bring my camping gear from home."

Yes, that's right, she thought then, relief storming through her. He'd told her earlier that the canyon wasn't his home. That he only visited. He probably wouldn't be here at all, or a least not very much, for the few days Maria was "getting to know her soul." She could handle an occasional meeting with him, she told herself. It wasn't as if she was some pubescent teenager who couldn't control her hormones. And she *did* have to buy those rugs. Lindsay would never forgive her if she came back without them. She could handle it, she decided. As long as John Redcloud kept his shirt on. . . .

She turned and looked directly at Maria. "I'd love to stay," she said with one of her dazzling smiles. "For however long you'd like to have me."

John stood abruptly, muffling a groan at her choice of words.

7

Only minutes after she said she'd stay, John left the *ramada* to stop a passing sight-seeing vehicle. Before Victoria quite knew how it had happened, he had her on it, still in her borrowed Indian garb, with her own clothes bundled in her arms.

"I'll pick you up at the lodge around five," he said brusquely. "Be ready." Then he stomped back through the cottonwoods to his grandmother's homesite.

Victoria made the ride to the lodge in piqued silence, her clothing clutched in her lap, chin up as she avoided the curious glances of the tourists who occupied the open-topped six-wheeler.

"I'll bet she doesn't speak any English," one of them whispered, and Victoria remained silent, content to let them think what they would. As soon as she was inside her room at the lodge she dialed her sister-in-law.

"Well, I don't know," Lindsay said when Victoria told her about Maria's wanting to "know her soul." "She never mentioned anything like that to me. We usually just had a cup of tea and a couple of these really delicious little corn cakes that she makes, while we discussed price and delivery dates and that's that. Although sometimes she invited me to stay and have dinner with the family." Lindsay paused. "Are you sure you understood her right, Victoria? Her English is pretty good, but it isn't perfect."

"Her English?" Victoria said. "I didn't even know she could speak English!"

"You didn't know she could speak— She didn't speak English to you at all?"

"Just a few words."

"Well, that certainly doesn't make any sense. Her English is quite—" She broke off as another thought occurred to her. "You didn't offend her in some way, did you, Victoria?"

"Lindsay!"

"Well, it's possible," Lindsay defended herself. "You might have offended some tribal taboo or something without even knowing it."

Victoria frowned into the phone. Had she done that? Had she done or said something that offended Maria Redcloud? But if she had, why would Maria ask her to stay for a few days? It didn't make sense. Still . . . "I suppose I could have done something," she said. "But I don't know what it would be."

"Tell me exactly what happened," Lindsay demanded.

Victoria told her, starting with her headlong tumble off the horse and ending with her trip to the outhouse with Christina. "And then, when I tried to bring up business, she said we had to eat first."

"I thought she didn't speak any English to you."

"She shoved a plate into my hands and said 'Eat.' Even I can understand that."

"Okay, okay. Don't get huffy. What happened next?"

"Nothing 'happened' next," she said, pushing aside the memory of John's hot eyes caressing her bare thigh. "We were just sitting there eating, and she suddenly decides that I need to stay in the canyon for a few days so she can 'know my soul.' She and John argued about it for a few minutes and then—"

"John?" Lindsay interrupted. "John who?"

"Her grandson," Victoria said, deliberately casual. "John Redcloud. He was acting as interpreter."

"She's got an army of grandsons." Lindsay chuckled. "And I can't imagine any of them daring to argue with her."

"Well, this one did. He—"

"Which one is he?" Lindsay interrupted again. "Describe him."

"Taller than average," Victoria said, picking her words with care. "Hazel eyes. He's only half Indian and—"

"Hazel eyes— Wait a minute. Are we talking about the hunk with all the muscles?"

"Well, I guess you could call him a hunk," Victoria conceded reluctantly. "He does have a fairly nice build."

"Fairly nice build! My God, Victoria, the man ripples when he walks. And that walk!"

"I'm sure Conrad would love to hear you talking about another man like that," Victoria said primly.

"Conrad can take it." Lindsay's warm chuckle came over the phone wires. "As long as all I do is talk. Is he going to be around while Mrs. Redcloud is getting acquainted with your soul?"

"I have no idea," Victoria said, forcing herself not to snap. "And less interest."

"Since when?"

Victoria ignored the question. "If his rippling muscles made such an impression on you," she said instead, "how come you never mentioned him after any of your buying trips?"

"Never came up, I guess. I met him the first time about, oh, four years ago I think it was, when he came back to the reservation for good after his divorce. And since then it's been just 'hello, how are you.' That sort of thing."

"How do you know he's divorced, then?" Victoria said, before she could stop herself.

"Well, as I recall, it was *the* topic of conversation all over the canyon that year."

"Oh?" Victoria said, hoping Lindsay would say more without her having to ask.

But Lindsay had known her for a long time. "I thought you weren't interested," she said teasingly.

"Lindsay..."

"Okay, okay. Well, the poop was, he'd been married to some gorgeous blonde he met in college. They were both majoring in computer science, or something like that, I think. Anyway—" Victoria could almost see her sister-in-law's airy wave. "After they graduated, he wanted to go back to the reservation and teach computer science at one of the schools there."

"He's a teacher?" No way could Victoria picture John Redcloud in a classroom full of students.

"I guess so, since that's what he wanted to do," Lindsay said. "But apparently his wife wouldn't go along with his plans. From what I gathered, she only visited the reservation once. Hated everything about it and refused ever to go back. One of Maria's granddaughters told me that it was no great loss, though. Except to John, I suppose," she added. "But none of his family liked her much." Lindsay sniffed delicately. "A real prima donna. You know the kind. So anyway—" Lindsay rattled on, barely pausing for breath "—he went to work for some big computer company. Fast-track yuppie stuff. Power breakfasting, dress for success and all that."

"I can't believe it," Victoria said, meaning John's Greek-god body hidden beneath a three-piece business suit.

"Yeah, I know what you mean. She sounds like a real spoiled bitch."

"No, I mean— Never mind. What happened next?"

"Haven't you been listening? They got divorced, that's what happened next."

"Well, is he teaching on the reservation?"

"I don't know, Victoria. I hardly know the man, after all." She paused. "Why don't you ask him if you're so all-fired hot to know?"

"Lindsay..."

"You could discuss teaching methods," Lindsay suggested. Victoria had earned a teaching degree in college. She'd never used it, but she had it. "Traditional versus Montessori." Her voice lowered. "Yours versus his."

"Lindsay..." Victoria said again.

"Oh, all right. I'll stop. I've got to go, anyway. Conrad will be home in a little while to take me to the doctor, and I'm not dressed yet."

"Is anything wrong?" Quick concern colored Victoria's voice.

"No, just a routine checkup. But my darling husband doesn't seem to think that I can get there by myself. He's driving me nuts with his constant worrying," she said, but there was a pleased note in her voice.

"Tell him to lighten up," Victoria suggested, knowing it wouldn't do any good. Conrad thought the sun rose and set on Lindsay's blond head. "Well, listen, I'll let you go so you can get dressed. I've got to change myself," she said, smoothing a hand over the wide skirt that pooled around her on the motel bed. "Take good care of yourself, Lindsay. And tell everyone to just expect me when they see me."

"I will." There was a slight pause. "You take care of yourself, too, honey, okay?"

"Sure," Victoria said, puzzled by the note of seriousness in her sister-in-law's voice. "Don't I always?"

"Sometimes I wonder."

"About what?"

"Oh, nothing." Lindsay sighed. "And everything. It's just that—" She hesitated for a moment. "Well, I just have the feeling that you aren't as happy as you pretend. A divorce is bound to leave some scars, Vics, even when it was as amicable as yours and Brad's."

"That was over eight months ago, Lindsay. And I'm fine. Really. There were no broken hearts, no unrequited love, not for either of us. We both wanted that divorce. We'd just been drifting along, living like brother and sister, for months before it finally happened."

"It didn't bother you when Brad remarried?"

"Lord, no!" Victoria said, and meant it with all her heart. "I'd have been happy to give the groom away if he'd asked me."

"But you seem, oh, I don't know. Restless, I guess. Like a . . . like a little lost child who's looking for something."

"Jeez, Lindsay, maybe Conrad's right to worry about you! You sound like you're having delusions or something."

"But—"

"No buts," Victoria interrupted firmly. "I'm fine. I'm not restless or lost or looking for anything that any other woman isn't looking for. So stop worrying; it's bad for the babies. Okay?"

"Okay," Lindsay said, but she didn't sound quite convinced.

Victoria hung up and bathed and changed and repacked, but she couldn't quite get Lindsay's words out of her mind. *A little lost child. Looking for something.*

Lindsay was right.

Oh, she didn't feel like a lost child, nothing so full of pathos as that. But she was restless. And looking for something. She'd have said "herself" but it sounded so self-indulgent and sixties. And it wasn't quite true. She knew exactly *who* she was; she had a strong ego and a well-defined sense of self. She just needed something to *do* with that self.

Something more important than golf with her father every Sunday and tennis with the "girls" twice a week at the country club, she thought, staring at her reflection as she flicked a blusher brush across her high cheekbones. Something more useful than passing out orange juice to donors at the local Red Cross blood drives. Something more interesting than shopping for clothes and going to parties and buying art for investment purposes. Something real and meaningful, she thought, leaning toward the mirror as she smoothed lip gloss on her mouth with her little finger.

Her restlessness was one of the reasons she'd agreed to fill in for Lindsay on the buying trip. She'd always like the desert. Liked its peacefulness and quiet, wild beauty. The stable where she boarded Ali was on the desert's edge so that she could ride into the peaceful silence whenever she needed to get away. Lately that need had become more and more frequent.

She'd thought that going on the buying trip, driving through all the wild, deserted areas of Arizona by herself without her friends and well-meaning family around to dangle distractions in front of her would give her lots of time to think. To plan. And to come to some decisions about her life.

But so far the only decision she'd come to was that things definitely had to change. What that change was, she still didn't know.

There was a sharp rap on her door then, startling her out of her introspective mood. She laid her hairbrush on the vanity next to her cosmetic case and went to open it.

John **stood** on the other side, one knee slightly bent, his hands lightly balled on his hips, his eyes shaded by his straw cowboy hat. "You ready?" he said, obviously not expecting her to be.

Victoria pulled open the door and stepped back. "I just have to put a few things in my cosmetic case," she

said, perversely pleased to be able to show him that he
was wrong. "That bag is ready to go, though." She
nodded toward the burgundy leather suitcase standing
at the foot of the bed.

A matching garment bag hung from the metal closet
rack next to the bathroom vanity. A few pieces of
clothing, airy dresses and skirts, hung next to it. Three
pairs of shoes stood on the overhead shelf. A paper-
back book lay facedown on the bedside table. Magazines and travel brochures were spread out over the
dresser. An emerald-green scarf floated over the back
of a chair.

She isn't ready, he thought with a kind of grim satisfaction as he stood just inside the threshold, survey-
ing the room. Well, he hadn't expected her to be. Hadn't
wanted her to be; being on time wouldn't have fitted
with the image he had of her. He lifted his gaze from the
green scarf, ready to issue a mocking remark on her
tardiness.

She was wearing jeans again. The faded fabric
cupped her bottom snuggly, almost lovingly, before
continuing down to outline each subtle curve of her
showgirl legs. A neat white silk-knit T-shirt covered her
narrow back, an elegant counterpoint to the denim
jeans. In the mirror he could see a small pocket over her
right breast. It jiggled as she fiddled with the items in
the cosmetic case.

John gave serious consideration to walking up behind her and putting his hand over that pocket. He
knew just how it would feel. Soft and small and firm
against his palm, the nipple burgeoning to life at his
touch. She'd be outraged at first—or pretend to be—but

he'd nuzzle through the silky hair at her neck with his cheek and whisper hot, sexy words into her ear until she melted back against him. The bed was only a step away. He'd lift her in his arms and put her down on the Indian-print spread and—

"There," Victoria said, fitting the last bottle into the case. "I'm ready."

John reined in his rampaging imagination with a hard jerk. "Not with all this stuff still left to pack, you aren't," he said curtly, still struggling with the image of her lying on the bed beneath him. His body was on fire.

"Yes, I am," she contradicted, looking up. "I'm—" Their eyes met in the mirror, locked for a breathless, heated second, then veered away. "It, ah, seemed silly to drag all this stuff out to the canyon," she said quickly, head down as she fumbled to close the cosmetic case. "So I'm keeping the room." She snapped the locks shut on the case and turned from the mirror. "It'll just be that one suitcase there," she said, sailing by him on her way out the door. She paused just outside the threshold of the room, her eyes anywhere but on him, waiting for him to bring her suitcase out so she could lock up.

Without a word, John picked up her suitcase and carried it out to his blue pickup.

Victoria closed the door behind him with a sharp little click.

"Better spread that horse blanket under this, Luis," he said, handing the suitcase to the man who stood up in the back of the truck to take it from him. He cast a derisive, sidelong glance at Victoria as she came up beside him, silently cursing her for being the object of his erotic imaginings. "It might get scratched otherwise."

"Please don't go to any trouble," Victoria said, smiling up at Luis as she handed up her cosmetic case. She ignored John. "It's survived the worst that the airlines can do. I'm sure a little jostling in the back of a truck won't hurt it any."

John tugged his hat down over his eyes. "Well, come on, let's get a move on. I—"

"Yes, I know. You have better things to do than stand around all day," she said, balking. "But I'd like to be introduced to your passengers first."

"Luis Redcloud," he said shortly, gesturing toward the back of the truck. "And his wife, Rose." He nodded toward the woman who sat cross-legged in the bed of the truck, her back against the cab, her hands curled loosely under the gentle swell of her stomach. "They're Ricky and Christina's parents. This is Grandmother's guest, Victoria Dillon."

"I'm very pleased to meet you," Victoria said politely, shaking her hair back as she smiled up at them. She wore pearl studs in her ears, creamy against the honey of her skin and the ebony fall of hair.

John pictured her wearing them and nothing else.

"I've met your children already," she continued, determined to win a response from the silent pair. "They're delightful. You must be very proud of them."

Two wide, shy smiles answered her. "Thank you," Rose said softly. Luis ducked his head in acknowledgment.

Victoria felt a rush of triumph.

The man beside her shifted impatiently.

"My sister-in-law is expecting twins in September," she said, ignoring him. "When is your baby due?"

Rose's hand caressed the small mound where her child lay. "In September also."

"Really?" Victoria took a step closer to the truck for a better look. "Lindsay's as big as a house already, and you look so—" She broke off, wondering suddenly if Navajos might not think pregnancy was an issue better discussed among women only. "Small," she finished, hoping she hadn't just violated a tribal taboo. Luis was looking distinctly uncomfortable.

Rose merely smiled. "It is different for every woman."

"Yes, of course," Victoria said.

"Are you ready to go now, little lady?" John said into the awkward little silence.

Her eyes flashed at that, as he'd known they would. That's why he'd said it. He owed her one, he thought, still smarting at the cavalier way she'd gestured toward her suitcase, as if he were a bellboy sent to carry it down to the lobby for her. Besides, it was the only way he knew to keep her—*himself*—at a safe distance.

"If you'd be so kind as to get out of the way," she said, her chin up.

He gave her a mocking little bow and stepped back, pulling open the passenger door of the truck. "Little lady," he said with mock gallantry, putting his hand under her elbow to assist her.

She jerked her arm away. "I'll ride in the back," she said, starting toward the tailgate. "Rose can sit in front."

John took her arm again, pulling her back. "Rose is fine where she is."

"But she's pregnant," Victoria hissed at him, trying to ignore the way the bare skin of her arm tingled un-

der his fingers. "She'll get all jostled around back there."
And I don't want to sit in front—alone—with you.

"No more than she would up front."

"But—"

"No buts, little lady. Rose is where she wants to be.
Get in." He propelled her into the cab of the truck and
closed the door with a bang. Victoria turned to face the
driver's side, ready to light into him the minute he
opened the door. There was a young woman sitting in
the middle of the bench seat.

She wore tan chinos, a crisp blue-and-white striped
shirt and a lightweight navy blazer. Her hair was a
dark, smooth sable brown, cut in a fashionable wedge.
Her eyes were lightly made up, set above exotic,
sharply angled cheekbones. Tiny gold hoop earrings
glittered in her ears.

"Hello. I'm Nina," she said, shifting the backpack on
her lap to offer her hand. "Another one of Maria Redcloud's grandchildren."

Victoria took her hand and smiled. "Victoria Dillon," she said, relief flooding through her as she realized that there would be a third person in the cab of the
truck.

"John tells us you'll be visiting with Grandmother for
a few days." She glanced sideways at John as he opened
the door on the driver's side of the truck. "He didn't tell
us why, though."

"Grandmother wants to know her soul," John said,
handing his hat to Nina as he slid behind the steering
wheel. His door slammed.

Nina turned to look at him more fully. "Her what?"

"Soul," he repeated, leaning forward to start the engine. "She wants to make sure her rugs will be treated with the reverence they deserve."

"But that's—I mean..." Nina's lovely black eyes were puzzled. "Is Grandmother playing some kind of joke?" she said in Navajo.

"Beats me," John said with a shrug. He shifted into gear without another word and headed the truck out the drive and down the road to the canyon.

Victoria was left wondering just what her two seatmates had said to each other. Obviously Nina found it a little unusual that her grandmother wanted to "know" Victoria's soul. But why? Did Maria only want to study the people she thought were lacking in some way? Did she like Victoria and want to know her better? Did she—

"What do you think of our canyon, Miss Dillon?" Nina asked.

"Call me Victoria, please." She smiled warmly. "I think it's lovely. So peaceful." She put her hand out, bracing it against the dashboard as the four-wheel-drive vehicle lurched over a rut in the shallow stream. "And the ruins are magnificent. Quite haunting, in a way. As if whoever left them might return at any moment to reclaim their property."

"Yes, I've felt that, too," Nina agreed. "Especially at night, when the moon is full and the shadows lie just so. Or at dawn, when the day has not yet started and it seems as if the Anasazi are inside sleeping."

John snorted. "You'd better not let Grandmother hear you say that," he advised.

"Why not?" Victoria asked Nina. "Doesn't your grandmother like the ruins?" She would be careful of mentioning them if that were the case.

Nina shook her head. "Grandmother is very old-fashioned and superstitious," she said, smiling. "She still believes in the old religion."

"That beautiful silver-and-turquoise cross she wears is just an ornament, then?"

Nina shook her head again. "Grandmother was sent to a mission school as a girl, and she believes in the Christian God. But she has merely added Him to the Holy People of the Navajo religion."

"Do the Holy People have something against the ruins?" Victoria asked, fascinated. She'd read avidly about the Navajo culture in her early teens, it had been a passionate interest for about six months, fading when she'd developed an equally passionate interest in boys. But it had never completely gone away. "Is that why you don't mention them to your grandmother?"

John snorted again and shifted to a lower gear. Victoria pretended that she hadn't noticed how the long hard muscles of his thigh moved under the material of his jeans. She also pretended that she'd never had that fantasy about the two of them entwined on this very seat.

"No," Nina said then, laughing a little. "No, that isn't why John advised me not to mention the ruins. It was the talk of the Anasazi still being inside. Or the thought that they might come back to reclaim what was theirs. You see, the old Navajo religion teaches that any of the Earth Surface People . . . We—all of us—" she circled her hand to include all three of them "—are the Earth

Surface People. And after death, if burial has not been performed properly or the burial site has been disturbed in some way, then the ghosts will come back to their former homes. And ghosts are the evil part of a dead person. Much feared by those who still believe in them."

"Oh, yes, I remember reading about that!" Victoria said eagerly, shifting on the seat so she could face Nina more fully. "The ghosts appear only at night, right? And they come back as..." She faltered a bit, her brow furrowing as she searched her memory. She didn't notice John's quick sideways look of surprise. "As coyotes and owls, I think."

"Yes. And as whirlwinds or dust devils or scurrying mice or simply dark shapes in the night," Nina said. "To a believer of the old religion, almost anything could be a ghost."

"Haunted houses," Victoria murmured then, gazing at the White House Ruins as they passed them. She suppressed a shiver, imagining them as they'd look at night with the moon casting ghostly shadows on the sandstone walls.

"No, not haunted houses," Nina protested with a laugh. "Just crumbling ruins."

"But you'd still better not mention it to Grandmother," John said, turning the truck out of the stream to park it near Maria Redcloud's hogan.

There was another pickup parked there already. A middle-aged woman in modified Navajo garb bent over the cook fire burning in the clearing between the *ramada* and the hogan. Maria Redcloud tended to the camp stove with Christina at her side. Ricky sat cross-legged in the shade of the *ramada*, playing some sort of game with a young man, whose shoulder-length hair was held back with a red bandanna, and an older man in a plaid Western shirt. All of them stopped what they were doing and turned to watch as the blue pickup pulled to a stop.

"Mama!" Christina hollered, flying toward the woman who was being helped out of the back by her husband. "Guess what I did today!"

Ricky was close on her heels, already jabbering his own version of whatever story Christina was telling.

John got a nod of welcome from the older man, a slap on the back from the younger.

Nina slipped from the truck and hurried over to be embraced by the woman at the cook fire, then turned to bestow a kiss on her grandmother's wizened cheek. She held out her left hand, displaying it for their approval.

Victoria waited by the truck, hesitant to intrude on the greetings of what was obviously some kind of family reunion. Why on earth had Maria Redcloud invited her to stay? She was beginning to be suspicious of the excuse that had been offered, but she had no idea what the real reason might be.

"Come and meet the family. Or part of it, anyway," John said in her ear.

Victoria started and looked up; she hadn't known he was so close.

"Hey, settle down," he said, offering his arm. "They won't bite."

Victoria stared up into his eyes for a moment, remembering what had happened the other times he'd touched her, wondering if she dared to let him touch her again. *Oh, what the hell*, she thought, exasperated at her juvenile imaginings.

"No, I'm quite sure they won't." She put her arm through his. "But will you?" she added in a provocative murmur, before she could stop herself.

John swore under his breath, cursing the impulse that had made him think she needed a friend in camp. Spoiled little twits like her never did; they'd been brought up to believe that everyone was just dying for their company.

THE MIDDLE-AGED WOMAN who'd been tending the fire was Dolores, Maria's youngest daughter and Nina's mother. The older man was Nina's father, Matt. The younger man with the long hair and the red bandanna was Dan, a cousin.

"At least you would call him a cousin," Nina told Victoria.

They were sitting side by side in the family circle under the *ramada*, feasting on roast lamb and a delicious casserole reminiscent of tamale pie. There were warm corn tortillas, too, and slow-baked beans and fresh summer squash and sun-ripened tomatoes that were unlike any Victoria had ever tasted. There was hot, strong coffee for the adults to drink and canned Cokes for the children.

"Dan is my mother's sister's son," Nina went on. "So, according to Navajo tradition, he is my brother."

"Does that make John your brother, too?" Victoria asked, glancing at him from under her lashes.

He was laughing, his head thrown back in appreciation of something one of the other men had said. The last rays of the evening sun snaked under the leafy roof of the *ramada*, gilding him with the soft red-tinted light that reflected off the canyon walls. His laughter gentled to a smile as she watched him. Absently still listening to the other man, he reached toward his plate. Lifting a piece of tortilla-wrapped lamb to his lips, he tilted his head and bit into it. His teeth were white and strong.

Chills chased down Victoria's spine. Would he bite a woman? she wondered, thinking of the muttered words they had exchanged by the truck. Was he the kind of man who would nibble on his lover, taking little love bites of her neck and shoulders, while his hands pleasured all the softest places on her body?

Suddenly, as if feeling her gaze, he turned his head. Victoria looked away quickly, refocusing her attention on Nina.

"So you see," she was saying. "Because John is the son of my mother's brother instead of my mother's sister, he and I are considered to be less closely related than Dan and me."

Victoria stared at her with a slightly glazed look in her eyes.

"I know it seems confusing to you," Nina said, misunderstanding Victoria's blank expression. "But the Anglo way of family relationships makes as little sense to us."

"Yes," Victoria said, still struggling with the fantasy that had taken hold of her. She could almost *feel* John's strong white teeth nibbling at her collarbone. "Yes, I suppose they must," she agreed, without the least idea of what they had been talking about. *Pull yourself together, Victoria!* "Does that mean..." She paused, struggling to come up with something that would sound as if she'd been paying attention. "Are Ricky and Christina your cousins too, or... or something else?" She focused her eyes on Nina's face, as if her answer was of the utmost interest. But her attention had already wandered back to the man sitting across from her.

She could feel him staring at her now, his amber gaze boring into her from across the food set out between them. She knew what she would see if she obeyed his silent demand to look at him. Hot amber eyes. Intense. Compelling. On the very edge of being totally irresistible.

So why are you resisting? she thought.

"... make it clearer for you?" Nina said next to her.

"Yes." Victoria nodded her head. "Yes, perfectly clear." She hadn't heard a word of what Nina said. "Thank you for explaining it to me."

Nina laughed. "Oh, that's my job," she said.

"Job?"

"I'm a teacher. Or I will be next fall."

"A teacher? Really?" Lindsay had said that John was a teacher. "Will you teach here on the reservation?"

"At Many Farms High School near Chinle."

She couldn't stop the question that rose to her lips. "Is that where John teaches?"

Nina shook her head. "John is a special case."

He certainly is, Victoria thought, sneaking a peek at him from under her lashes. He was still looking at her. She shifted her gaze back to Nina.

"He is not a teacher, not formally," Nina said. "He is a computer software expert. But he teaches computer literacy at three schools on the reservation. Many Farms High School is one of them."

"How interesting," Victoria murmured encouragingly.

"We do not have many computers yet. And those we do have are not the newest, but John feels that it is vitally important that our children step into the future with the rest of the world. So he drives his traveling classroom around to the different schools and continues to petition the council for more and better equipment."

"Traveling classroom?" Victoria said, fiddling with the rim of her empty plate.

"It's just a big van, really," Nina explained, "set up like a miniature classroom. It is John's dream to one day have many such vans and many teachers who will use the newest and best computers to teach our students. He says that—" She broke off as Maria rose from her place in the circle to begin clearing up the dishes. "Let me do that, Grandmother," Nina said, coming to her feet. "You sit back down and relax."

Victoria set her plate aside. "Can I help?" she said, also beginning to rise.

"No, please." Nina waved her back down. "You are the guest of our grandmother. Rose and I will see to the cleaning up."

"You're sure? I'd be happy to help. I—"

"You want to help so bad," John said from across the circle, "you can come and help me."

Victoria looked into the amber eyes she had been trying so hard to avoid. They were as hot, as intense, as compelling as she had known they would be. "Help you?" she said suspiciously. "How?"

"Your tent has to be set up before it gets too dark to see." He rose in one fluid motion. "You might as well give me a hand with it."

"I don't know anything about putting up a tent," Victoria said, stalling.

"Then it's about time you learned, isn't it?" He stepped across the circle, reached down, grasped her by the upper arms and hauled her to her feet. "Lesson number one," he said quietly, staring down into her face. "Everybody pulls their own weight around here. Even women like you."

"Women like me?" she said, insulted by the implication that she wasn't willing to pitch in. She'd offered to help with the dishes, hadn't she? "What do you mean, 'women like—'"

But John had turned away from her, heading for the camping gear in the back of his truck. Fuming, Victoria followed him.

8

"JUST WHAT DO YOU MEAN 'women like me'?" she hissed at his back. "What kind of woman do you think I am? And what gives you the right to judge me, anyway?"

He turned and shoved a rolled sleeping bag into her arms. "You're a spoiled rotten, useless parasite," he said stonily, more angry at himself than her. He'd been sitting there at dinner, salivating over her while she had just done what came naturally, charming everyone in sight with her easy smile, inflaming him past all reason. "An extremely decorative one, I'll grant you that." He turned back to the truck. "But still a parasite."

"Parasite?" Victoria sputtered. "*Parasite!*" Her voice rose from an angry hiss to an outraged squeak. Heads turned. She lowered it with an effort. "Just who the hell do you think you are, calling me a parasite? You don't even know me," she charged in a furious whisper, refusing to acknowledge the part of her mind that said he just might be right. She'd been feeling pretty useless lately. "You don't know who I am or what—"

He turned around again, his own arms full of camping gear. A lantern dangled from one hand. "I know all about women like you." He moved to brush past her.

Victoria stepped to block his path. "You know nothing about women like me," she informed him haughtily, her chin in the air. The sleeping bag was clutched to her chest like a shield. "Chauvinistic, Greek-god egomaniacs like you never do. If you took a minute to look at a woman as a person instead of some brainless sex object, you'd—"

"Is that what you think I think you are? A brainless sex object?"

"Do you deny it?" she challenged him.

John ran his eyes over the classically elegant lines of her upturned face—the narrowed eyes with their black-lace lashes, the lips firmed in anger, the jaw set, the pulse beating furiously at the base of her throat.

Brainless? No, she wasn't brainless. Intelligence was evident in every beautifully sculpted line of her face; it burned behind those spitfire eyes. But intelligence without purpose was useless. Worse, it was dangerous. It led to boredom and mindless acquisitiveness and mischief making merely for the sake of something to do. He'd had his fill of bright, bored, materialistic women who couldn't see beyond their own wants. He only wished this particular one weren't so damned beautiful. He couldn't breathe properly when he looked at her. Couldn't stop himself from imagining what it would be like to have her . . . keep her.

"Well?" she demanded, unnerved by his stare but determined not to show it. Why was he looking at her like that? "Do you deny it?"

"Do I deny what?" John said softly, bemused by the way her lips curved around her words. Such soft lips. Sweet lips. Kissable, rose-red lips.

Victoria took a cautious half step back. Why was he looking at her like that? "Do you deny that you, umm, think of me as, ah . . ." She trailed off, licking her lips as John leaned forward slightly. Was he going to kiss her? Oh, she hoped he was going to kiss her! Unconsciously, completely forgetting her anger and the rest of the Redcloud clan, she clutched the sleeping bag closer to her chest and lifted her chin.

John caught himself before his mouth touched hers. *What in hell are you thinking about?* he demanded silently, pulling himself back with a jerk. The lantern banged against his knee. *What the hell are you thinking with?* Not his head, surely. Hadn't he told himself that he wasn't going to get anywhere near her? Hadn't he promised himself while he was driving out to his place to get the camping gear that he was going to treat her like any other visitor to the canyon? Casual and friendly but distant. Yet here he was, on the very verge of necking with her—with most of his family sitting not forty feet away, pretending not to notice while he made a fool of himself.

"Sure, I see you as a sex object," he tossed off casually. Keep her annoyed with him, he thought. Keep himself annoyed with her. It was safer that way. He shifted the camping gear in his arms and stepped around her. "Same as you see me as one. We haven't known each other long enough to get beyond the physical."

Victoria's teeth snapped closed. "The same as I see you? I don't see you as a— Hey, don't walk away from me when I'm talking to you," she demanded, turning to trot after him. She reached out and grabbed his arm. "I do not see you as a sex object."

He lifted an eyebrow. "Don't you?"

Victoria dropped her hand. "No, I don't," she lied, falling into step beside him. They headed toward a stand of cottonwoods and peach trees, away from Maria Redcloud's homesite. Several moments passed in silence.

"So how do you see me, then?" John said, slanting a look at her out of the corner of his eye.

"Well, I see you as . . ." How *did* she see him? Visions of his bare, sweaty chest flickered through her mind. Remembered dreams flushed her cheeks. "As I said before, I think you're a chauvinistic, ah—" *Greek god* had been the words she'd used; she hoped he wouldn't remember them. "—overbearing egomaniac with Neanderthal tendencies."

"I think I heard the words 'Greek god' in your description the last time," he taunted mildly.

"Dream on," Victoria scoffed, staring straight ahead.

"You're going to deny you said that?"

"Yes."

John considered that for a moment. "Probably a wise move," he agreed, nudging her off the path. "Here we are."

"Here we are where?"

"Your campsite."

"What's that?" She nodded toward a small hogan made of logs and mortar. "A storeroom?"

John set the lantern down, then knelt, tumbling the rest of the camping gear to the ground. "That's my hogan."

"Your hogan?" It sat less than twenty feet from where he had dumped her camping gear. "Don't you stay with your grandmother?"

"This is my grandmother's land—the clan's land," he corrected. "There are several hogans on it. Grandmother's. Mine." He began unfolding the tent as he spoke. "Rose and Luis and the kids have one on the other side of the outhouse. Matt and Dolores are right through that stand of cottonwoods there. We Navajos like our privacy."

"So why are you setting my tent up practically at your front door?"

John didn't even look up. "Someone has to keep an eye on you." He had the tent spread completely out, hurrying before the rapidly increasing dusk made it impossible to see clearly. "I'm it."

"I don't need anyone to keep an eye on me."

"Uh-huh." He stood. "Mind giving me a hand with this?"

Victoria dropped the sleeping bag to the ground and went over to help him. "I don't need anyone to keep an eye on me," she said again, mostly just to needle him. She was still irked by that parasite crack.

"Hold this right here." He put a long, curved metal tube in her hand. One end sat on the ground, the other arched high over what would be the center of the tent. "Don't try to move it," he cautioned. "Just hold it so it doesn't go anywhere. I've got to go around to the other side and attach it."

The tube wobbled in her hand as he positioned the nylon fabric and lightweight metal supports.

"Hold it still," John commanded.

Victoria grasped it with both hands. She heard a click, then a sliding sound as two metal tubes fitted together.

"One more," John said. Another tug, another click. "There." The tent ballooned up as if by magic, a green nylon igloo supported by four curved aluminum poles. "That's got it."

"I don't need anyone to keep an eye on me," Victoria said again as John came around from behind the tent.

"I heard you the first time." He knelt down by the pile of camping gear. Opening a green drawstring bag, he pulled out a rubber mallet and four tent stakes.

"But you didn't answer me."

"Because I didn't hear a question. Here." He handed her three of the stakes. "Hold these."

Victoria took them with a loud, put-upon sigh. "I could do this myself, you know," she said, standing behind him as he anchored the first corner of the tent. "I went to summer camp when I was a kid," she told him, watching his shoulder bunch and flex under the material of his shirt as he hammered the stake in. "I'm not completely useless."

He pounded a second stake into the ground, then turned and looked up at her. "Be my guest." He offered the mallet.

Victoria backed away with a look of shock on her face and shook her head. "I might break a nail," she said in a wispy little voice. "And, what with no manicurist around, it might be *days* before I could get it fixed. I'd be helpless. Absolutely helpless."

John grinned at the ground. "I'm sorry I called you a parasite, all right? I shouldn't have said it."

She noticed he didn't say anything about the spoiled rotten epithet. But she'd give him that; she was spoiled. She handed him the third stake. "But you meant it."

"No I didn't. I was just mad." Two hard whacks of the mallet secured the stake. "You're probably very good at whatever it is you do for a living."

Victoria stifled the urge to admit that she didn't do much of anything for a living.

"Here in the canyon, though, you're a fish out of water," John went on, moving around the fourth corner of the tent as he spoke. Victoria trailed along behind him, watching as he pulled the nylon material taut with one hard tug. She handed him the last stake before he could ask for it. "You stick out like a high-priced—" he whacked the stake with the mallet "—pampered—" another whack "—Thoroughbred mare in a field of plow horses," he said, pounding the stake right into the ground. "There, that should do it." He stood, turning toward her as he rose.

They were nearly nose to nose. *Or nose to throat*, Victoria thought. His was brown and strong. "Is that why you were mad?" she asked, her voice suddenly low and husky. Why was it that every time she got close to him her voice changed?

"Mad?" he echoed vaguely, drinking in the heady scent of her perfume. Night-blooming flowers and forbidden sex. You had to be close to her to smell it, though. Really close. He liked that.

"You said you called me a parasite because you were mad," she said softly, mesmerized by the smooth triangle of coppery skin visible between the open buttons of his shirt. She wondered if it was as smooth as it looked. If it tasted as warm as she imagined it must. "At me? Because I don't belong here?"

"At you?" He lifted his hand, realized he still held the mallet, and dropped it again. The mallet slipped from his fingers. Unable to stop himself, he raised them to her hair. It was as soft and slippery as silk fringe. "No, I wasn't mad at you. Not really."

Victoria's eyes drifted upward, over his jaw and the strong, square chin with its intriguing suggestion of a cleft, to his mouth. That tender, sensual mouth. "At who then?" she murmured, not even realizing that she'd lifted her hand to his shirtfront.

"Myself, I guess." His fingers feathered through the hair at her temple, his thumb brushing across the skin of her cheek. She was satin smooth, velvet soft. Fragile as a hothouse flower.

"Why?" Her hand slid up his shirtfront until her fingertips just touched the bare skin of his upper chest. It was warm and hard. Unyielding as the canyon walls that rose up around them. She could feel his heart beating beneath her palm. "Why?" she said again.

"Because I wanted you." He curled his hand around her nape, urging her forward. Her head fell back, cradled in his big palm, her silky hair sliding through his fingers. Her eyes were wide and shining, staring up at him through the gathering dusk. "*Want* you," he corrected, his voice a husky caress. His other arm went around her back, bringing her to him. "And I shouldn't," he said. But he bent his head, anyway.

Their lips met hungrily, the heat rising up between them with brushfire speed, just as it had the last time. Victoria had no time to think, to consider, to evaluate. She merely responded. Just as she had the last time. Only more so. Her body surged forward, her arms reached out, her head tilted, her mouth opened, her tongue met his. *Do with me what you will*, she thought as she melted against him. *Take me*, she thought. *Love me*. Did she say it aloud?

John's response was as instantaneous as if she had. And as overwhelming. He felt himself harden everywhere; his arms, his thighs, his sex all tightened with an almost painful intensity. He wanted to drag her down to the ground right then, that very instant, and drive himself into her yielding softness. But he wanted everything else, too. He wanted to explore the heady, intoxicating flavors of her mouth, to test the softness of her breasts with his palms, to trace all the delicate bones of her body with his fingertips, to taste the fragrant skin of her throat and shoulders and breasts. He wanted . . . wanted . . . wanted.

Too much.

It was too much. And not enough. It would never be enough. She would drive him crazy before it was enough.

"Victoria," he said against her mouth.

"Yes," she murmured, not knowing whether she asked a question or made an offer.

"Victoria, this is crazy." His lips went on a reckless journey across her cheek.

"Yes," she said again, arching her neck sideways so that he could reach her ear.

His tongue rasped against her lobe, over the tiny pearl stud. "We shouldn't."

"I know." Her lips pursed against his chest, her tongue darting out to taste him. "We don't even know each other."

He groaned and pressed her closer. "I promised myself I'd stay away from women like you," he said, his mouth against the soft skin where her neck curved into her shoulder.

"And you're not even my type," she assured him, nuzzling into his throat. Her hands kneaded the fabric of his shirt like a kitten at the breast.

"We should stop." His lips covered hers again, tasting, nibbling, teasing with hungry openmouthed kisses.

"Yes . . ." Their heads turned and tilted, seeking new angles, new pressures. Their tongues touched and parted and touched again. "Yes . . . we've got to stop this."

"So stop me," he demanded unsteadily, unable to stop himself.

Victoria moaned and took a deep, shaky breath. "Stop," she said, letting it out. Her hands stilled against the fabric of his shirt. "John, stop."

He stopped, his forehead coming to rest against hers as they fought to steady their breathing, his hands holding her shoulders, her palms resting on his chest. A second later he lifted his head. "I'm sorry, Victoria, I—"

She put a finger to his lips. "No, don't ever say you're sorry for kissing a woman. Not when she's already kissed you back." She took another deep breath and stepped away from him, out of his embrace. "Just say 'thank you very much' and go."

He hadn't been going to apologize for kissing her, but for calling her names. Still, maybe it was better to let her think that. "Go?"

"Please," she said, not quite meeting his eyes. "It's been a long day, and I think I'd like to go to bed."

He nodded, then gestured toward the jumble of camping gear on the ground behind them. "Let me finish setting up camp for you."

"All I need is the sleeping bag. I think I can manage to unroll that by myself."

"You'll need the air mattress, too. And some light. It's going to be pitch dark in about ten minutes." He knelt down to the lantern, adjusted the wick and lit it. "You can take this inside the tent with you when you're ready," he said, rising. "Just be careful with it. Make sure it's completely off before you go to sleep."

"I will."

"You know how to adjust it?"

She nodded. She'd watched him just now. "Yes."

"Okay." He found himself reluctant to leave her. She looked so little, standing there in the glow of the lantern. So fragile in her tight jeans and designer T-shirt. Totally unable to take care of herself even in this tame wilderness. He had to forcibly restrain himself from taking her in his arms again. "There's a flashlight in that bag," he said gruffly, pointing. "You'll need it if you have to make a trip to the outhouse. The air mattress is rolled up inside the sleeping bag. You sure you don't want me to blow it up for you?"

"I'm sure. It may take me a few minutes," she added when he continued to hesitate, "but I'm reasonably sure I can blow it up myself."

John nodded. "All right. If you change your mind about going to bed, come on back to the *ramada*.

There'll be story telling and singing for a couple of hours yet."

Victoria was already kneeling by the camping gear. "I won't change my mind," she said, head down as she began to untie the cords that held the sleeping bag rolled up. "Good night."

"Good night."

He was gone.

Victoria's hands stilled on the sleeping bag and started to shake instead. She'd never responded like that before. Not to any man. Never felt hot and cold and shaky all at once. Never wanted someone so quickly. So passionately. So desperately. So much so that she'd have lain down for him right then . . . if he'd asked her. It was frightening.

She hardly knew the man. No, dammit, she didn't know the man at all! A day and a half ago she hadn't even known he existed. And she didn't even like him. Not really. He was arrogant and chauvinistic and . . . and judgmental. And he didn't like her, either. He'd called her a parasite. True, he'd taken it back. But he'd said it, so he must have meant it. And he didn't want to want her. It made him mad at himself to want her. "I shouldn't," he'd said, just before he kissed her.

She didn't want any part of a grudging passion! She deserved better than that.

But he was so beautiful. Physically, he was the most beautiful man she'd ever seen. Those amber eyes. That talented, sensual mouth. That smooth, coppery chest, so warm under her fingertips. Those hard, callused hands that had touched her face so gently, with such exquisite care.

He'd touched Ricky and Christina with the same gentleness, she remembered. He'd hauled the little boy up onto the back of his horse without hurting him, carried the little girl on his shoulders. He was a gentle man, despite his size and obvious strength. He had humor; she'd seen it gleam in answer to her own more than once. He had compassion and loyalty; any man who'd come back to live and teach on the reservation when he could so obviously make a good living in the outside world had to have a goodly supply of both. He had—

Stop it, Victoria, she chided herself then. *Just hold it right there.*

She knew what she was doing. Rationalizing. Justifying. Giving herself reasons to give in to the frenzied passion he generated in her. But it wasn't going to work.

You're leaving in a few days, she reminded herself. *A week at most.* As soon as Maria Redcloud satisfied herself on the condition of her soul and agreed to a price on the rugs, she'd be gone. Never to return again.

Victoria wasn't the kind of woman who indulged in brief, meaningless affairs—she'd only ever slept with two men, her ex-husband included—and she wasn't going to start now. Certainly not with a man who thought she was a spoiled rotten, useless parasite!

She stood up, bundling the sleeping bag and air mattress in her arms, and ducked into the tent. It was roomy inside, six feet by six feet at least, maybe more, and high enough for her to stand up in the center. The tough nylon fabric continued onto the ground, forming a floor that protected her from any creepy crawlies or dampness. She dropped the bedding next to the wall of the tent and went outside for the rest of the gear. She brought the lantern inside next, setting it by the open flaps so it would continue to shine some of its light outside. All that was left was the green drawstring bag with the flashlight and whatever other camping gear it held. But no suitcases. They were still in John's truck.

Well, she didn't need them, Victoria decided reluctantly. She could forgo brushing her teeth for one night. She could be extra thorough in cleansing her face tomorrow before she redid her makeup. And she could sleep in her teddy. It wouldn't kill her. She'd get the suitcases in the morning.

That decision made, she turned to making up her bed. The air mattress was a sturdier kind than one might use to float on in a pool. Harder to blow up. She was red in the face by the time she'd decided it had enough air in it to sleep on. She placed it on the floor against the wall of the tent and spread the sleeping bag over it. It looked comfortable enough, she decided, testing it with her hand. A little soft and soggy maybe, but she preferred a soft bed.

She dragged the green drawstring bag into her lap and opened it. A tin plate, cup and cutlery set, two small towels, two washcloths, a canteen, a little round can of bug repellant ointment that smelled awful when she opened it to take a sniff, a small packet of tissues, a Swiss army-type knife with lots of little attachments, a box of wooden matches, a computer manual and a flashlight. In case she had to make a trip to the outhouse. She did.

She got up and poked her head out of the tent. It was full night out now, the cottonwoods and peach trees tall ghostly shapes in the blackness, the pale slice of moon giving off a wavering light. Off to her right, in the direction of Maria's hogan, she could see a light glowing through the trees. Lanterns, she thought, and, perhaps, a campfire. To her left, in the direction of the outhouse, was only darkness.

How badly did she have to go? Badly, she decided, and it would only get worse if she put it off, because she would lie there in the sleeping bag and think about it. Shining the flashlight back and forth in front of her, she headed down the path to the outhouse.

It never got this dark in the city, she thought, stepping carefully. So dark that you could barely see your hand in front of your face. And quiet. She had never heard such quiet. No traffic, no sirens, no televisions or radios. Just the faint rustle of the breeze in the trees and the scurrying noises of—

She stopped in midstep, swinging the flashlight to shine on the bushes and trees that bordered the path. Something scuttled away from the light. A creepy feeling crawled up her spine.

Snakes? she wondered fearfully. Lizards? Something larger and furrier with big, ugly teeth? Something otherworldly? She decided she didn't want to know. Turning the light back onto the path, she hurried toward the outhouse as fast as she dared over the uneven ground. She used the facility quickly, propping the flashlight on the floor, then hurried back to her tent, the creepy feeling hunching her shoulders the whole way. Only iron willpower kept her from running.

Safe, she thought, ducking into the tent. She moved the lantern away from the entrance and zipped up the flap to keep out whatever furry little beasties might be lurking in the night. It was all cozy and private inside with the sleeping bag against the wall and the lantern glowing in the corner and the night locked out behind the tent flap. Nothing to be afraid of. And nothing to do now but go to bed. It was hours earlier than her normal bedtime but, surprisingly, she was tired. As she'd said to John, it had been a long day.

She leaned down, turning back the top of the sleeping bag, then stood up, pushed off her tennis shoes with the toe of the opposite foot and reached for the zipper on her jeans.

JOHN STOPPED, STOCK-STILL in the shelter of the trees, a burgundy suitcase in either hand, and stared at the sight that greeted him. She was inside the tent, her body in profile to him, the lantern on high, undressing. She toed off her shoes, giving a little kick to fling them away from her as they slipped off her heels, and reached for the zipper on her jeans. She undid the waistband button first. Then, with the thumb and finger of her right hand, she grasped the zipper tab and pulled it down. Slowly, so slowly, it seemed, although it only took her a second. Her hands lifted then, and slipped inside the loosened waistband to push the jeans down her legs. Her long, endless, showgirl legs. The descending jeans revealed them reluctantly, almost lovingly—those firm luscious thighs, the rounded knees, the shapely calves, every line, every curve showing up in sharp relief, larger than life, as her shadow flickered on the nylon tent. She bent from the waist, her right knee, and then her left, lifting as she pushed the jeans off over each foot. She straightened and shook the jeans out, folding them in half and then in half again, before dropping them on the tent floor. Her hands crossed over her torso, reaching for the hem of her T-shirt.

John's mouth went dry and his hands on the handles of the suitcases began to sweat. *Look away, you pervert*, he told himself. But he couldn't.

She pulled the T-shirt up over her head, exposing the lines of her firm, flat stomach, her delicate ribcage, her breasts. They were on the small side. But not too small, he thought, staring at their shadowed outline on the tent. They were delicate and elegant, like the rest of her, with sweet tip-tilted little nipples that—

She wasn't wearing any underwear! Of its own volition, his gaze dropped to the juncture at the tops of her thighs. The way she was standing, with the light behind her and every little detail magnified he should be able to see . . . but he couldn't. Underpants, then, he thought, though why it mattered, he didn't know. But at least she was wearing underpants. The thought calmed him.

She shook the T-shirt out, folded it loosely and knelt to place it on top of the jeans. Without straightening, she turned and knee-walked across the tent to the lantern, enlarging and distorting her image on the wall of the tent. The light flickered but didn't go out.

John took a firmer grip on the suitcases and moved forward, making enough noise so that she would be sure to hear him. He saw her shadow jump, her hair swing against her shoulder as she turned her head toward the sound.

"Victoria," he called before she could have time to get frightened. His voice came out froggy. He cleared it. "It's John Redcloud. I've got your suitcases."

"Oh, good, my suitcases." She jumped up, turned toward the flap of the tent, then hesitated. "Ah, wait a minute. I'm not dressed." She scurried toward the meager pile of clothes she had just taken off. "I have to get dressed."

"Just get into the sleeping bag."

"What?"

He had to clear his throat again. "Get into the sleeping bag and cover up. I'll bring the suitcases in."

"Oh . . . Oh, okay. Just a minute. Let me unzip the flap." There was a long rasping noise, the scurry of feet. He watched her blurred image wiggle into the sleeping bag. "Okay. You can come in."

He ducked into the tent. It was cozy, a bit warm from being closed up with the lantern on high. But maybe that was just him. "I thought you might need these before morning," he said, setting the cases down in the middle of the tent. He tried not to look at her. He tried not to even think of her. Naked but for those ridiculous bits of ribbon and lace she called panties, snuggled down in his sleeping bag, in his tent. It was more than a bit warm in here, he decided. It was damned hot.

"Thank you for bringing them," Victoria said. "I'd resigned myself to doing without them until morning."

He nodded and turned to go.

"Ah, before you leave . . ."

He halted, his hand on the tent flap, and looked over at her. She was sitting up, the sleeping bag held to her chest with one hand. "What?"

"The lantern," she said sheepishly, gesturing toward it. "I can't figure out how to turn it off."

"I thought you said you knew how."

Her shoulders lifted. Her eyes dropped. "I lied," she admitted. "I thought I could figure it out."

He picked up the lantern, swinging it in an arc as he turned toward her. "Here," he said, crouching beside the sleeping bag. "Watch me."

Victoria watched. His big hands. The denim pulled tight across his thighs by his splayed knees. The metal buttons on the fly of his jeans. She wondered what he'd do if she put her hand on his thigh. High on his thigh, and then slid it all the way up to where those metal buttons strained at the fabric of his jeans. Would he stop to think about how he "shouldn't" then?

"Got that?"

"Oh . . . yes." Her eyes flickered up to his then down again. "I think." A guilty flush touched her cheeks. She hadn't seen a thing he'd done. "Could you show me once more? Just so I'm sure?"

"Yeah, sure. Once more." Mechanically he went through the explanation again, showing her where to light the lantern with one of the wooden matches, how to turn it down or off, all the time sneaking peeks at the smooth bare skin that showed above the edge of the sleeping bag. She was wearing something on top, after all. There were narrow, honey-colored lace bands lying over both shoulders, almost the same shade as her honey-colored skin. He wondered what she'd do if he reached over and pushed them down. And then pushed her down, flat on her back in his sleeping bag, and covered her body with his own. Would she kiss him the way she had before, all wild and honey sweet? Would she be able to summon the will to tell him to stop?

"Thank you," she said then, softly. "I think I can do it now."

He hadn't even been aware that he'd finished the demonstration. He stood, anyway, leaving the lantern where it was. "You should turn it down to about a fourth of what it is now when you're getting undressed at night," he advised, looking down at the top of her bent head. The part in her hair was precisely placed. It made him want to mess it up.

"Why is that?" Victoria stared at the lantern.

"Otherwise it throws your shadow up on the wall of the tent."

She looked up. "My shadow?" Her eyes widened with comprehension. "On the wall?"

He gave her that smirky, condescending, know-it-all male grin. "It was a helluva show, little lady," he said, lifting the flap of the tent. "A helluva show."

9

THE HEAT WOKE HER. She'd zipped the tent flap up again after John left and now, with the sun striking directly on the green nylon, it was stifling inside. She had wriggled out of the sleeping bag sometime during the night and lay on top of it, but a fine sheen of perspiration covered her body. She sat up groggily and pushed her hair off her face with one hand. She wasn't a particularly cheerful riser at the best of times, nor an early one, but she was awake now, with little chance that she'd be able to roll over and go back to sleep, so she decided that she might as well get up. She needed air. Rolling to her hands and knees, she crawled over to the tent flap, unzipped it and stuck her head out.

It was a beautiful morning. The most beautiful morning she could remember seeing in a long time. Sunlight glinted off the steep walls of the canyon, giving a faint, magical red glow to the fresh morning light. A slight breeze rustled through the trees, bringing her the scent of juniper and woodsmoke and—she sniffed deeply, appreciatively—coffee. A bell, the kind worn by milk cows and goats, tinkled rhythmically somewhere off through the trees to her left. A child laughed.

She pulled her head back inside the tent and flipped open the top of her large suitcase, looking for clean clothes. A quick trip to the outhouse, she thought, an equally quick sponge bath, a light dusting of makeup and she'd be ready to face the world—and the Red-cloud clan.

THERE WERE ONLY WOMEN in Maria Redcloud's *ramada* as Victoria approached it. Maria, her granddaughter Nina and her great-granddaughter, Christina. Only seven o'clock in the morning, Victoria marveled, and already they were all busy at some task. Maria sat before her loom, stringing it in preparation for a new weaving. Christina was carding wool. Nina sat cross-legged, her head bent as she plied a needle through the mound of white fabric in her lap.

"Good morning," Victoria called when she was near enough to do it without shouting.

Nina and Christina looked up from their work and smiled. Maria glanced around and nodded. "Good morning," Nina greeted her. "Did you sleep well?"

"Like a baby," Victoria lied. She'd spent the night fighting dreams of John. "Am I too late for coffee?"

"I will get it for you," Christina offered.

"No, stay where you are. I can get it." Victoria set the borrowed skirt and tunic she was carrying on top of a large covered basket. "One of these cups okay?"

Nina nodded, ducking her head to bite off a thread with her teeth. "There is sugar and powdered creamer there—" she pointed "—if you want them."

"Black is fine," Victoria said, pouring a cup from the enameled coffee pot that sat simmering on the camp stove. She came over to sink cross-legged onto the sheepskin where Nina and Christina sat. "Is that suede you're working on?" she asked, nodding toward the white fabric in Nina's lap.

"Yes." Nina held it up for her to see. It was a tunic, shaped much like the one that Maria was wearing, but with a long fringe on the hem. Embossed silver, coin-like buttons decorated the long sleeves and outlined the split collar. An intricate pattern done in tiny blue and coral beads covered three-fourths of the bodice. It was this that Nina was working on.

"Oh, how beautiful!" Victoria gasped, reaching out to touch it.

"My wedding dress," Nina said proudly.

"Your wedding dress?"

"I am to be married next week."

"Congratulations," Victoria said warmly. "Or is it good luck one wishes the bride? I can never remember." She smiled at Nina over her coffee cup, recalling that she had seen Nina extend her hand to her mother and grandmother last night after greeting them. Showing off her engagement ring, of course. It suggested that her family hadn't seen it before; which suggested that Nina didn't live in the canyon and was only here to prepare for her wedding. So why in heaven, Victoria wondered, would Maria Redcloud want a stranger around in the midst of her granddaughter's wedding preparations?

"Your ring—" Victoria nodded toward the intricately wrought silver ring on Nina's left hand "—may I see it?"

Nina held out her hand. The ring featured a highly polished, intensely blue turquoise at its center, surrounded by diamond chips. Unusual and lovely, it was the perfect blending of the old world and the new.

"It's exquisite."

"Thank you," Nina said proudly. "My fiancé made it especially for me. It is one of a kind."

Maria Redcloud turned from her loom then and spoke to her granddaughter.

"Yes, Grandmother. I'm sorry," Nina said in Navajo. She turned to Victoria. "Grandmother reminds me that I haven't offered you any breakfast. I can prepare you—"

"No, nothing," Victoria interrupted her. "Coffee is more than enough."

"You're sure? It would be no trouble."

"Positive. I never eat in the morning."

Maria spoke again, a rapid string of Navajo, scolding in tone. Nina replied in the same language.

"Humph," Maria said and turned back to her loom.

Nina laughed. "Grandmother says you are too thin," she said to Victoria. "I told her it is the fashion to be thin. You can see her response."

Victoria smiled at the old woman's back. "My father feels the same way," she said. "He's always trying to put fried potatoes on my plate when I eat at home. Well—" She put her empty coffee cup aside. "What can I do to help?" She wriggled her hands in front of her. "Two free hands with nothing to do," she said.

"Really, there is nothing," Nina assured her. "You are our guest."

Maria spoke from her loom. Nina looked toward her, startled by whatever she had said, and asked a quick question. Maria repeated herself. Nina shrugged.

"Grandmother suggests that you might like to help Christina card her wool," Nina said.

"Oh, yes, I'd love to." Victoria scooted across the sheepskin rug. "If Christina would show me how," she said, smiling at the child. "I've never done it before."

Christina transferred the wooden cards to Victoria's lap and patiently showed her the motion to make. It was harder than it looked, the scraping motion requiring a certain pressure and rhythm to do it just right. Victoria flubbed it; Christina laughed and showed her again, and then again until she was finally doing a credible, if painfully slow, job of carding the wool.

"In a little time," Nina said approvingly, her needle flying through the suede cloth in her lap, "you will be nearly as good as Christina."

They whiled away the morning that way, talking and sewing and laughing. Victoria learned that the rest of the Redcloud family had risen with the sun. Nina's mother, Dolores, her sister, Rose, and her brother-in-law, Luis, all worked at the lodge. Her father, Matt, was off on council business. John and Dan and Ricky were mending a fence and doing other "man things" Nina said, making a face to show that they were probably mostly goofing off. Victoria heard about Nina's fiancé, Bob, who was a teacher like herself, as well as being a skilled silversmith.

In turn she told them of her own teaching degree and about Lindsay's pregnancy and her husband's almost comic concern for her, and she made them laugh with a story about a mishap her mother had had with the new fertilizer for her prize-winning orchids.

The pile of carded wool by her side grew slowly but steadily, giving her an immense sense of satisfaction, all out of proportion to the task. Sitting there in the shade of the *ramada*, sharing work and idle woman-talk of weddings and babies and families, she felt completely content and relaxed for the first time in a long time—and not at all restless. Which was strange, she thought, since she hadn't made any progress at all toward the task that had brought her here in the first place.

"I don't know when I've enjoyed myself more," she said when Nina set her beadwork aside to start preparations for the noon meal.

"But you must have many good times," Nina said, lifting a large three-legged "spider" skillet off of the hook that suspended it from the ceiling of the *ramada*.

"Yes," Victoria agreed. "But not like this." She spread her arms wide. "The canyon is so beautiful. So peaceful. And—" she smiled down at Christina "—the company so congenial. It's like a whole 'nother world here." She paused thoughtfully. "A better world, maybe."

"You sound like John," Nina said. She moved to the clearing and placed the skillet securely over the white-hot embers of the cook fire. "Every summer when we Navajo move back into the canyon," she said over her shoulder, "he says the same thing."

"Back into the canyon?" Victoria got to her feet and ambled over to lean a shoulder on one of the *ramada's* supporting posts so they could talk more easily. "Don't you live here all year?"

"No, only in summer. It gets very cold here in the wintertime. Too cold. And the children must go to school."

"So where do you live? In the winter, I mean?"

"In Chinle. At least, most of us do. Many of my cousins are still in college, so they go off to school in the cities. Some of them live in the city permanently." She poured oil from a large square can into the skillet, then lifted the lid of a large ice chest. "As John did until four years ago. He has a house outside of Chinle now, toward Many Farms." Chunks of meat, chicken from the looks of it, sizzled in the pan. "It's a ranch, really. He is building a fine herd of horses. They are his first love. More than his precious computers, even."

Maria commented then, from her seat in front of the loom.

"Yes, Grandmother," Nina agreed in English. "Horses are much better than computers. We Navajo," she said to Victoria, "have historically counted our wealth in sheep and horses." She cast a fond smile at her grandmother. "Grandmother is slow to give up the old ways."

"The horses John raises," Victoria said, "Arabians?"

"I don't know." Nina shrugged. "They are horses." She wiped her hands off on a dishtowel and sprinkled salt over the meat frying in the pan. "Christina, go call the men to lunch, please. Tell them they have plenty of time to wash up before it is ready."

The child gathered up the carded wool that she and Victoria had accumulated, storing it away, then scampered off to do as she was told.

Victoria pushed herself away from the pole. "Is there something I can do to help with lunch?" she asked, remembering John's comments last night. Spoiled rotten. Useless parasite. She didn't want him to catch her hanging around doing nothing while everyone else was busy doing something productive.

"No, nothing—" Nina began, but Maria cut her off. Nina shrugged. "Grandmother says you could pick some tomatoes from the garden. And perhaps some yellow squash for the evening meal if enough are ripe."

She handed Victoria a large basket with handles on either side. "The garden's right up there," she said, pointing.

The tomatoes proved to be no problem; anyone could tell a ripe tomato from an unripe one. She picked six big fat juicy ones, holding them to her nose to sniff before laying them in the basket. Nothing in the world smelled like vine-ripened tomatoes. The supermarket variety didn't even come close.

She walked between the rows of growing things, brushing carefully past tall stalks of corn and low, rambling pumpkin vines, to the squash. Yellow squash, Nina had said. They all looked to be varying shades of yellow to Victoria. Pale yellow crookneck. Yellow-green patty pan. Two other varieties that she didn't recognize at all, except that one of them looked like bright yellow zucchini, the kind that she was used to seeing dark green in the grocery store. Did that mean it wasn't ripe? Were any of them ripe? She couldn't tell.

She stood indecisively in the middle of the garden, afraid to pick anything for fear it would be the wrong thing. The crookneck *looked* as if it was ripe to her. But maybe not. Most of them were small and pale yellow, and wasn't crookneck bright yellow when it was ripe? The only thing to do was go back to the *ramada* and ask. It was embarrassing to be so stupid about such a simple thing, but it would be more embarrassing to pick the wrong squash and bring back a basket of unripe, inedible vegetables. They were to be for dinner, anyway, Nina had said, so it wouldn't delay lunch any if they weren't picked right now. Hefting the basket to her hip, Victoria started back down to the *ramada*.

JOHN WATCHED HER AMBLE down the gentle incline from the garden. It seemed all he had done for the past two days was watch Victoria. Watch her move. Watch her sleep. Watch her undress. It was becoming addictive.

She carried a basket on her hip, as naturally and casually as Rose or Dolores or Maria herself might carry it. He didn't stop to think that women—all women—had carried burdens like that since time began—baskets of garden produce, sacks of groceries, babies. He only saw that she did it as if she had been doing it all her life, just like the other women here. Even her clothes, if one didn't look too closely, contributed to the illusion that she belonged.

Like Nina, she wore shorts. They were khaki shorts, fashionably baggy and rumpled, belted with Italian leather and topped by another of those silky little T-shirts, but still shorts. There were dusty tennis shoes on her sockless feet and a smear of mud on her left knee from where she had knelt in the garden. He found himself wondering if she was wearing that honey-colored scrap of lace underneath.

She stopped short of the *ramada*, veering off to speak to Nina where she stood over the cook fire, turning meat with a long-handled fork. She extended her basket with a little shrug and a smile and asked a question. Nina laughed softly and shook her head.

"No matter," John heard her say. "Christina will get them later."

Maria rose from her place in front of the loom at that, demanding in Navajo to know what the problem was.

"It's nothing, Grandmother," Nina assured her. "Just that Victoria wasn't sure which squash to pick. Christina can do it later, after we have eaten."

With a gesture, Maria demanded to see the basket. Silently Victoria handed it to her. Maria lifted out a tomato with a gnarled hand, raised it to her nose and sniffed. Nodding grudgingly, she put it back in the basket. "Where are the squash?" she said in Navajo, stabbing a bony finger into the mostly empty basket.

"I told you, Grandmother," Nina answered in the same language, "Victoria wasn't sure which squash were ripe."

"How can a grown woman not know when food is ready to be picked?" Maria said loudly, casting a sly, satisfied look toward the men sitting in the shade of the *ramada*.

John suddenly realized what his grandmother was up to. She didn't want to "know" Victoria's soul at all, she wanted to show it—expose it—to him. Victoria was a city woman, an Anglo, non-Indian, and Maria wanted to make sure that John knew it. She knew—somehow, she knew!—how strongly attracted he was to her. She wanted to nip that attraction in the bud, show him that it was as unsuitable as his last disastrous attraction to an Anglo woman had been.

Oh, Grandmother, John thought. *I know it's unsuitable. I don't need you to point it out to me by making Victoria feel inadequate.*

Maria gestured to Christina, calling the little girl to her side. "Please show our guest how to tell which squash is ripe," she instructed her. She tumbled the tomatoes into a bowl, handed the basket back to Victoria and waved them both toward the garden. Victoria, feeling like a chastised child, followed the little girl.

AFTER A LUNCH of fresh corn tortillas, sliced garden tomatoes and fried rabbit—which, Victoria was happy
to note, tasted a lot like the chicken she had thought it
was—it was time to wash up. Victoria, guest or no
guest, found herself helping. Not that she minded
helping. She wanted to help. She found it interesting to
see how women washed up with no electric dish-
washer, let alone no running water. It was even fun, in
a way, washing the enameled dishes in water pumped
from a well and heated over an open campfire. It wasn't
as if she, or they, had anything else to do that washing
the dishes interfered with or kept them from doing. It
was simply the next thing on the agenda, and they did
it, as they had done everything that morning, with a
spirit of camaraderie and burdens made lighter by
sharing.

And then Victoria broke a nail. Reaching into the
soapy bucket of water for a plate, she snapped the nail
off all the way to the quick. The plate slipped through
her fingers and clattered to the ground. Victoria
clutched the wounded fingertip with her own hand and
pressed it against her middle, trying not to howl at the
sharp, stinging pain.

"What is it, Victoria?" Nina asked, alarmed. "Did
you cut yourself?"

"No, no." Victoria released her finger, waved it in the
air as if to cool it, then clutched it to her again. "It's
nothing."

John looked up from the length of leather strap he
was repairing in the shade of the *ramada*.

Maria's hands hesitated at her loom.

"Let me see," Nina said, reaching for her hand. "How
bad is it?"

"Grandmother!" Christina hollered, scrambling for the fallen plate. "Victoria has cut herself."

John rose to his feet, stopping only long enough to assist Maria to hers as he headed toward the commotion around the wash tub.

"It's nothing really," Victoria insisted. "I didn't cut myself. It's just . . ." she paused, staring at the four concerned faces staring back at her. "It's just a . . . broken nail," she finished sheepishly, feeling like a prize fool. She held it out to show them.

The nail on the index finger of her right hand was gone, torn off just below the quick. No blood showed, no gore, just one glaringly broken nail among four long, perfectly manicured, gleaming red ones.

"All that noise for a broken fingernail?" Maria said incredulously in Navajo, slanting a pleased glance up at her grandson to see if he had seen how silly the Anglo woman was acting. He had.

"Looks like you'll live," he said dryly, that irritating, indulgent-male smile on his face as he turned back to the *ramada* and the leather strap he was mending.

Nina was more sympathetic. "Here," she said, handing Victoria the dishtowel. "You dry. It will probably sting if you put it in the water."

SHE BROKE THE SECOND NAIL pulling weeds in the garden. It wasn't a painful break this time, just annoying, and Victoria glanced at it only long enough to note that her manicurist was going to have a fit when she finally got back to Phoenix.

At this point it was anybody's guess as to when that might be. Maria had steadfastly refused to discuss the sale of her rugs, claiming, when Victoria had tried to talk to her through Nina, that she still did not properly know her soul. And then she had sent her off with Christina to be shown how to weed a garden.

It turned out to be fun, and deeply satisfying, too, to dig her hands into the rich, giving earth. She began to understand why her mother spent so much time fooling with those orchids of hers. But how much better, Victoria thought, when the fruit of your labor was food for your family rather than some exotic flower that had no use beyond its beauty. She thought briefly of starting her own vegetable garden when she got back home and then discarded the idea. It wouldn't be the same as this garden; she'd be working it by herself, with no one to share it. Much of the enchantment of weeding a garden, she discovered, had to do with whom one shared the chore.

Christina proved to be a delightful companion. Talkative now that she had lost her shyness with Victoria, she chattered on about her family and her school and her summers in the canyon.

"I have six sheep of my own," she informed Victoria as they crept along on hands and knees, pulling weeds from between the rows of vegetables. "Grandmother adds one more every year because I am to be a weaver like her. And like the Spider Woman."

"Spiderwoman?" Victoria asked, thinking of the comic-book character.

"A long time ago," Christina began, repeating a legend she had been told dozens of times, "when the Navajo had just become Earth Surface People, the Spider Woman taught us how to weave."

"And Spider Woman is one of the Holy People," Victoria said, remembering more of what she had once read.

"Yes," agreed Christina. "She lives on top of Spider Rock in the canyon," she added matter-of-factly. She sat back on her heels and wiped a small, grimy hand across her face. "Now it is your turn to tell a story."

Victoria obliged, regaling a wide-eyed Christina with the story of Snow White. She didn't think any more about her nails that afternoon, not even noticing when a third one planted itself in the earth.

IT WAS DARK, the evening meal had been eaten and cleared away, and the various members of the Redcloud clan had retired to their respective hogans. Victoria sat alone just inside the open flap of her tent with her cosmetic case beside her and a pair of nail clippers in hand, calmly cutting off what was left of her nails. She'd already taken off the red polish, sucking in her breath when the remover stung the tender, exposed quick on her index finger.

Her hands looked a little odd, she thought, holding them out in front of her when she'd finished clipping the nails. Odd, but not *too* awful—except for the jaggedly torn nail on her right hand. When she got them all filed smooth, though, they'd be fine. Not glamorous anymore, by any means, but serviceable, which she was beginning to think was better.

She dropped the clippers into the little plastic pouch by her side and picked up a nail file. Head bent, knees crossed Indian fashion, her billowy white cotton nightgown pooled around her thighs, she sat in the soft light cast by the lantern, humming lightly under her breath as she filed her nails.

She had never known such . . . such tranquillity, she thought, sighing as she smoothed the edges of the first nail. Never had such a sense of satisfaction from a day's work before. Which might, she thought, smiling to herself, have something to do with the fact that she'd never *done* a day's work before. Not really.

As the beloved only daughter of Emily and Thomas Cullen of Cullen's Department Store and the cherished baby sister of Conrad Cullen, she'd found life had always been effortless and easy. She had, she knew, been shamelessly catered to and pampered all her life. From babyhood on, her parents, her brother, even the family servants had seen to it that she'd had what she wanted almost before she knew she wanted it. School had been easy; she'd never had to sweat for the B average that followed her all the way through college. Friends had been easy; both sexes seemed predisposed to seek her out for companionship. Love and marriage had been easy; she'd met Brad Dillon during her junior year in college, become engaged in her senior year and married him in the wedding of the Phoenix social season after graduation. Even the divorce had been easy.

And none of it had given her the same sense of satisfaction and accomplishment that she'd gained from one day of doing manual labor. She was tired, she marveled, actually physically *tired* from something more than just dancing all night. It was, she discovered, a wonderful feeling. The only thing that would have made it more wonderful was someone to share it with. Someone like John.

She hadn't seen him since the embarrassing "incident of the broken nail" as she had started thinking of it. He had taken his mended leather strap off to wherever it was he intended to use it, and not returned for the rest of the day. Not even for dinner.

"John and Dan have gone into Chinle for more fence wire," Nina had said, explaining their absence.

Victoria spent the evening wondering if it took all day and half the night to buy fence wire. She wondered, too, if he were avoiding her in the hope that he wouldn't have to be witness to any more of her silly little calamities.

Sure, she thought, she'd made a fool of herself a couple of times that day. First when Maria had so summarily sent her off with six-year-old Christina to show her how to pick ripe squash, and again when she'd made such a stupid fuss over her broken nail. But she'd done much better later, weeding the garden without mishap, trying her hand at a bit of simple basket weaving without making a complete botch of it, helping with dinner without burning herself or anything else and later, after the evening meal had been cleared away, she'd even contributed to the communal story hour by telling the tale of Icarus and his wax wings to highly favorable reviews. She had even, once or twice, caught Maria looking at her with an expression of grudging respect.

It would have been nice—the icing on the cake, so to speak—if John had been there to see that she wasn't entirely useless.

But he wasn't. So she'd gone off to her tent without the satisfaction of being able to send an I-told-you-so look in his direction. Well, maybe tomorrow, she thought. Yes, definitely tomorrow.

She'd be sitting there in the *ramada*, competently carding wool or working on the simple yucca basket Nina had helped her start and telling some educational sort of story to Christina as she worked. John couldn't help but be impressed with the picture that would make, she thought, smiling in anticipation as she filed her nails. Or maybe he'd show up just around lunchtime, and she'd be patting bread dough between her hands, forming neat little ovals for frying as Maria had done for tonight's supper. Or maybe she'd be—

"You're looking very pleased with yourself," John said, making her jump.

Well, speak of the devil, she thought, looking up to find him standing just outside the tied-back flap of the tent, one knee slightly bent, hands on hips as he stared down at her. His eyes gleamed golden. His dark brown hair was slightly damp, as if he'd just washed. His shirt was unbuttoned, revealing the little charm around his neck. Victoria's heart started to beat double time.

"Where'd you come from?" she said, trying to sound cool and unruffled. She casually resumed filing her nails, as if his mere presence hadn't rattled her right down to her toes.

"Chinle." He tried not to look at her bare knees. Her bare shoulders. The little lace ruffle that adorned the sleeveless bodice of her white nightgown. He'd tried not to stop here at all, intending to go straight to his hogan after washing up. "I saw your light when I came down the path," he said a little defensively, "so I thought I'd deliver a message from Willie Salt."

"Willie Salt?" The file hummed furiously over her nails.

"The service-station mechanic."

"Oh, yes. My car." She stopped filing as a terrible thought occurred to her. Her eyes as she looked up at him were those of a disappointed child. "Is it fixed?"

"Yeah," John said, wondering why the hell she was looking at him like that—as if he'd just taken away her favorite doll. "Willie says you can pick it up tomorrow. I thought you'd be pleased."

"Well, I am...I guess. I mean, I'm glad the car's fixed. But—" She brightened suddenly. "I can't get it tomorrow. Your grandmother and I haven't come to an agreement on her rugs yet. We haven't even agreed to discuss it. I can't leave until we do," she said with satisfaction.

"Grandmother will come to an agreement fast enough if she knows you're set on leaving."

"But I'm not! I mean— She wants to 'learn my soul,' doesn't she? To make sure her rugs are treated with the reverence they deserve. I couldn't leave before she was sure of that."

John snorted. "You don't really believe that tripe, do you?"

"Well, yes, of course I do. Why else would she want me here?"

"Why else, indeed?" he said dryly, turning to leave. If he stayed, he'd end up telling her more than he should. Or worse.

Victoria jumped to her feet. "Hey, wait a minute." She stepped outside the tent, heedless of her bare feet, and put out a hand to stop him. "You can't say something like that and then just walk away."

He looked down on the hand on his arm. Small, delicate, elegant even without the long red nails; it was burning a hole through his sleeve. "I think it would be better if I did," he said.

"Well, I don't! I want to know what you meant."

"You do, do you?" he responded, amused in spite of himself by her imperative demand. Standing there in her nightgown, barefoot, coming only to his chin, she was as imperious as a queen on her throne. John fought not to be delighted by it.

"Yes, I do! Why would your grandmother want me here, if not for the reason she gave?"

John hesitated. *What the hell*, he thought. *Tell her.* It would give her something to think about besides herself. "My grandmother," he said, "wants you here to prove to me that you're no good."

"*What?*" she bristled. "What do you mean, 'no good'?"

"No good for me," he elaborated.

"No good for you...?" Victoria's eyes widened in the darkness as she looked up at him. "I don't understand."

Unable to resist, he reached up and caught her chin between his thumb and finger. "It's very simple, really," he said, staring down into her eyes. Her beautiful, fiery, melted-chocolate eyes. "My grandmother knows I'm attracted to you. She knew it the minute she laid eyes on you. The good Lord only knows how, but she did. And she knows what happened the last time I was attracted to a woman like you."

"A woman like me?" Victoria whispered. "Why do you keep saying that? What kind of woman is a woman like me?"

"A city woman. A pampered, spoiled Anglo woman."

His wife, Victoria thought. *He's talking about his wife.*

"Grandmother thought a little reminder of how unsuitable a woman like you is to this life—the Navajo life—my life—was in order. So she decided to keep you around for a few days to show me just how poorly a woman like you fits in."

"Stop saying 'a woman like you'!" she said, jerking her chin out of his hand. "I'm not any *kind* of woman." *I'm not like your wife.* "I'm me." She didn't know why it was so important to make him see that, but it was. Desperately important. "I'm an individual. So don't try to shove me into some narrow little pigeonhole, because I won't fit."

"No," he agreed softly, fighting the need to take her in his arms and kiss away the frown between her chocolate eyes. "I guess you won't, at that. Nina said that you'd enjoyed yourself today, despite the damage to your hands," he added reflectively, as if he'd just remembered what his cousin had told him. "She said you actually seemed to get a kick out of weeding the garden."

"I did," Victoria assured him quickly. "I liked it a lot."

"It doesn't change anything." He lifted his hand and ran the back of his finger slowly, wistfully, down her cheek. "I still can't have you."

Something stilled in Victoria's chest. Her heart, she thought. And her lungs. All the vital functions ceased for one incredible, momentous second. And then they started up again. Beating harder, taking in more air than they ever had before. *"I still can't have you,"* he'd said.

But he could. Oh, he could!

Because she loved him. Just like that, standing there in the darkness, it hit her like a fist in the solar plexus. Less than seventy-two hours after she'd first looked into his amber eyes she knew, beyond any doubt or hesitation, that she loved him. She realized immediately that it wasn't going to be effortless or easy, the way everything else in her life had been. But it was going to be worth it, the way nothing else had ever been.

"John, I . . ." she began, not really knowing what she was going to say, only knowing that she had to express this feeling that had burst alive inside her.

"No, don't say it," he cautioned, shaking his head. "I know you want me, too. But it wouldn't work. We're too dif—"

"No, that's not it at all! Well, it is, partly," she admitted because it was. "But—"

He put his finger over her lips. "No," he said again when she tried to speak. "Just go back inside your tent and go to bed. Forget we ever had this conversation."

Victoria went, but there was no way she was going to forget. Forget the most important, the most wonderful thing that had ever happened to her? Not likely. One little no wasn't enough to discourage Victoria Dillon. Not even a hundred noes would discourage her now. Not when she finally knew what it was that she wanted in life.

"Just you wait, John Redcloud," she said, smiling at the ceiling of her tent as she lay there on his sleeping bag. "Tomorrow you won't know what hit you."

10

"AND THAT ONE IS MINE," Christina said, pointing to a deceptively sleepy-eyed sheep that looked no different to Victoria than any of the other thirty-odd sheep they had just herded into the newly mended wire-enclosed corral. "And that one, too," she added, indicating a smaller, fatter sheep penned up alone in a separate corner of the corral. It stood there doing what it had apparently been doing all morning—eating. "It is the one we will serve to the guests at Nina's wedding," she said proudly.

"How nice," Victoria said, trying not to pant. She was still a bit winded—all right, she amended silently, a *lot* winded—from chasing uncooperative sheep in directions they didn't want to go. She'd been given a "simple" job to do, one that, it was pointed out to her, was routinely relegated to small children.

"Just stand right there," Christina had said, obeying her great-grandmother's instructions to let Victoria help with herding the sheep back into their pen. "Just wave your arms if one tries to run by you."

They all tried to run by her. Every single blasted one of them. Dumb as they looked, they were apparently smart enough to sense ignorance and inexperience and, Victoria admitted to herself, a little fear. Did sheep bite?

They didn't bite, it seemed. At least, none of them tried to bite *her*. But they dodged and darted and feinted with all the expertise of an LA Raiders' running back. And Victoria was no lineman. She waved her arms and shouted and screamed and ended up chasing more than one of them into the bush until she got it turned around and headed back in the right direction.

Didn't shepherds have dogs to do this sort of thing?

"It is my wedding present to Nina," Christina said, still talking about the sheep penned up by itself, "because it is my sheep. Grandfather," she added, referring to Nina and Rose's father, Matt, "will butcher it, and Mama will roast it with herbs over a big fire for all the guests. We will have corn pudding, too," she said, smiling up at Victoria. "Do you like corn pudding?"

"I don't know." Victoria had her breath back now and could return the smile. "What is it?"

"You don't know what corn pudding is?" Christina said, aghast that anyone, even an Anglo, was unfamiliar with the Southwestern delicacy.

"It's a sweet dessert, something like custard," said a deep musical voice from behind them.

Victoria whirled around, a bright smile on her face. "John!"

He returned her greeting with a wary nod, his amber eyes moving down her slim form, taking in the disheveled hair, the dusty shorts, the soaked sneakers that she'd earned by chasing sheep through the stream. A quick, unwilling grin turned up the corners of his mouth. She looked like a ragamuffin. "Having fun?"

"Oodles and oodles."

"We've been herding the sheep back in the corral," Christina said excitedly. "You should have seen Victoria! She jumped up and down and hollered so loud."

Christina demonstrated, waving her arms wildly. "And she chased them and chased them. It was so funny!"

"I'm sure it was," John agreed, smiling down at his niece. "But it's not nice to laugh at someone else's mistakes," he chided gently, reaching out to soften the reprimand by smoothing the child's hair with his palm.

"But Victoria laughed, too!" Christina said.

John flicked a quick glance at Victoria's face. "She did?" Clearly, he didn't expect her to have laughed at anything that had gotten her damp, dusty and sweaty.

Victoria shrugged. "I appreciate a good joke as well as the next person," she said, irked that he would think she was so lacking in humor that she couldn't laugh at herself. Hadn't they already shared a smile or two themselves? "And it *was* funny." She gave John a wry look. "I'm only sorry your grandmother wasn't here to appreciate it."

"I'll tell her," Christina volunteered, skipping away from them. "I'll tell her." She came to an abrupt stop, turned and came back to look up at Victoria from under silky brown lashes, her round eyes serious. "Can I tell her?" she asked, mindful of her uncle's warning about making fun of other people's mistakes.

"Sure," Victoria said, ruffling the child's hair. "You tell her." With a shout, Christina rushed off. "I'm sure it's only what she's expecting to hear, anyway," she added under her breath.

"You don't have to put up with all this, you know," John said as they followed more slowly after Christina.

"Put up with what?"

"This." He lifted an arm. "Chasing sheep. Weeding the garden. Carding wool. Grandmother fully intends to sell you the rugs no matter what."

"I'm not 'putting up' with anything," Victoria told him. "I'm enjoying it immensely."

"Yeah, sure." He tried to ignore the smiling face that said she was, indeed, enjoying it and glanced down at her hands. "You've ruined your nails."

"No!" she drawled. "Do you really think they're ruined?" She held her hands out in front of her, inspecting them as if she had been unaware of the damage before now. Her hands looked strong and capable to her. Useful. She liked the change. "My nails were too long, anyway," she said carelessly, dropping her hands to her sides.

"You're shoes are soaked."

Victoria shrugged. "Cooler that way."

"You've torn your shorts."

Victoria didn't even look down. "Old shorts," she said.

John came to a stop and stared down at her. Victoria stopped, too, and smiled up at him with an expectant look in her eyes. There was a streak of red dust on her cheekbone. A small twig was caught in her tangled ebony hair. The glow of perspiration dampened her flushed cheeks. And still, somehow, she managed to look as elegant and unconcerned and as pleased with herself as if she had just stepped out of the most exclusive beauty salon in Phoenix.

She was so damned different from what he'd expected her to be—from what he needed her to be if he was going to be safe from her . . . charms. By all rights she should have been whining about her hair and her nails and the hole in her designer shorts. She should have been complaining about the lack of running water and indoor plumbing and the fact that Maria Redcloud had turned what was ordinarily a cut-and-dried business deal into some sort of endurance test. Dammit, she should have hightailed it back to her room at the lodge after the first night! But no, she was still here in the canyon, to all appearances, quite simply having fun.

"You really are enjoying this, aren't you?" he said, his tone hovering between amusement and annoyance. He didn't want her to be enjoying it, dammit! But he was glad she was.

"What's not to enjoy? Fresh air. Good food. Good company. New experiences." *You.* She didn't say the last word, but it was there in her eyes.

It was the same look she'd given him last night. A promise; an offer; a plea almost. He couldn't tell, exactly, but it tugged at something deep inside him, something dangerous. He looked away, clearing his throat, and stuffed his hands into the back pockets of his jeans to keep from reaching for her. *Lust*, he said to himself. *It's just lust.*

"Yeah, maybe," he said, and started off toward the *ramada* again. His posture, his walk, his expression reminded Victoria of nothing so much as a sulky little boy who wanted something he thought he couldn't have. She smiled fondly at his broad back, fully expecting him to kick the ground with the toe of his boot.

He pulled up short instead, turning his head to look at her when she didn't immediately follow him. "I told Willie I'd get you over there this afternoon to pick up your car," he said gruffly. "So let's get a move on." An eyebrow arched, indicating her rumpled condition. "I

have more important things to do than wait around all
day for you to get cleaned up."

WELL, THOUGHT VICTORIA, *alone at last in the front
seat of John Redcloud's blue pickup truck with only his
straw cowboy hat on the seat between us.* She looked
over at him, half hoping that he'd make her fantasy
come true and fall on her like a starving hound on a
bone. More than hoping. Wanting. Desperately.

"What?" he asked, feeling her stare.

Victoria forced her eyes forward. "Nothing," she
said, a small, secret smile curving her lips. If he knew
what she was thinking he'd probably be shocked right
out of his boots. And then, again, maybe not. "I want
you," he'd said, and then he'd kissed her with a passion
that sent her head spinning every time she thought
about it. *"Stop me,"* he'd said, unable to stop himself.
Maybe he was having a few fantasies of his own.

He was.

He could sense the feelings radiating from her like
heat waves in the desert. The same feelings that sizzled
through him. *Lust*, he reminded himself, his hands
tightening on the steering wheel. *Just lust.* They'd been
frothing with it ever since they first set eyes on each
other. At least *he* had, and it had been building, higher
and hotter, ever since, until all he could think about was
pulling this heap over to the side of the road and taking
her on the front seat. It would be a frenzied coupling.
Their straining bodies half-clothed and slicked with
passion. Their breathing harsh. Their hearts pounding
in unison.

He should have brought Christina along, he thought
then, shaking his head to dislodge the image of their

two bodies locked together in heated abandon. A child sitting on the seat between them would have kept these feelings, these fantasies, at bay. He wouldn't have been tempted to act them out. Oh, hell, he thought. Tempted. Always tempted. But he couldn't have done anything with Christina in the truck. And this way he could; there was nothing to stop him. Not even Victoria.

Because she was receptive to him. All right, more than receptive. She was as hot and bothered as he was. And it was driving him crazy because he wasn't— dammit, he *wasn't*—going to give in to it. To her. It would only be asking for trouble.

Thank God the service station was only a few miles down the road. He could drop her off; let her get her car; be rid of the temptation to ravage her for the rest of the afternoon.

The gas station was closed. At least, the garage was. And Victoria's flashy little car was locked inside for safekeeping. A young teenager, not more than fourteen years old, was tending the gas pumps.

"Willie had some kinda emergency," he informed them. "Closed up everything but the pumps. I don't know where he keeps the key to the garage or when he'll be back. He didn't say."

"Damn it all," John swore, banging his hand against the hood of his truck. "Now I'll have to take you back to the canyon before I can go out to my place."

"Your place? The ranch Nina told me about?"

"Yeah, I need to go out and check on a few things. I was going to drop you off, let you drive yourself back to the lodge. Oh, well, hell," he sighed, resigning himself to another fifteen minutes of temptation tearing at his guts. "Get in. I'll take you back. You can check on your room, take a shower or a nap or something. I'll pick you up after I've finished at the ranch."

The idea of a shower was very tempting; she hadn't been wet from head to toe, all at once, for a couple of days. But the thought of seeing John's ranch—spending the afternoon alone with John—was even more tempting.

"I'd rather go out to your place with you," she said.

"My place?" John felt a bead of sweat trickle down his back as he thought of her there, at his place, in his house. Not a good idea. "What the hell for?"

"I'd like to see it. Nina said you raised horses."

"Yeah. So?"

"Well." Victoria shrugged. "I want to see it, that's all."

"And do you always get what you want?"

"Mostly," she answered honestly. "Unless there's some good reason I shouldn't." She paused. "Is there?"

"Is there what?"

"Some good reason I shouldn't see your ranch."

He could think of a dozen good reasons, all of them beginning and ending with this . . . this *feeling* they had for each other. "No, I guess not. Okay, get in. We'll go out to the ranch."

THE HOUSE WASN'T AT ALL WHAT she was expecting. Although exactly what she was expecting she couldn't have said. A large log hogan, maybe, or something closely resembling one. But the long dirt road they traveled down after they left the two-lane blacktop highway ended in front of the kind of low, rambling ranch house one might see anywhere in the southwestern United States. The outside was native stone and timber with a wide, rough-hewn plank deck running across the front and around one side, and a double carport with a big yellow van parked under it on the other. A hay barn, horse barn and neat network of corrals were spread out behind the house. It looked like what it was—a working ranch.

Victoria was delighted. "This is wonderful, John," she said, slipping out of the truck. "I had no idea it would be like this." She looked around, not knowing what to explore first. If everything worked out the way she wanted it to—hoped it would—this would be her winter home. The thought made her want to hug herself. Or him. Yes, definitely him. But he was standing on the other side of the truck, hands on his hips, watching her with a wary expression on his face, unaware of the plans swirling around in her head. "Can I see the horses? The house?"

"There's the house," he said, waving his arm. "The horses are down this way."

"I meant the inside."

"Of what?"

"Of the house, of course. What else would I mean?"

"What do you want to see inside the house for?" he asked suspiciously. He didn't want her in the house! If she went in the house—if he saw her standing inside his house—there wouldn't be any corner of his life left that he didn't somehow associate with fantasies of her.

"Well, it's usually considered polite to invite a person inside your house." She thought she understood his reluctance, considering his past experience with Anglo women, but it wasn't as if she was going to steal the silver or anything.

"In the Anglo world, maybe. We Navajos are a little more choosy about who we let in."

"Oh," she said softly. "Well, if you don't want me in your house, then . . ." her voice trailed off.

Damn! Now she looked as if he'd stolen her doll again. "Look, if you want to see the inside of the house, it's fine with me," he said.

Her face brightened instantly.

"Well, what'll it be?" John said irritably. "Horses first, or the house?"

"Horses," she said, sensing that would please him. Nina had said that horses were his first love. They had been her number-one interest, too, until last night. "I'd love to see the horses."

"Well, let's get a move on then," he groused. "Get it the hell over with." He headed out in the direction of the corrals, his long stride swallowing ground.

Victoria had to hustle to keep up with him. "Hey," she panted after a moment. "Hey, slow down."

He shortened his stride. "Sorry." He'd forgotten that as long as her legs were, they weren't as long as his. "Better?"

"Yes, thank you." Victoria smiled up at him and tucked her hand through his arm as if they were strolling along a downtown sidewalk instead of sending up little puffs of dust with every footfall on the way to the barn. "Tell me about your horses," she invited him.

Automatically John crooked his elbow, giving her a better handhold. But he held himself stiffly, careful not to press her hand against his side as every nerve in his body screamed at him to do. He was dying to feel her hands on him, even so casually. "What do you want to know?"

"Everything. How many horses do you have? How long have you been raising them? Do you show them? What kind of breeding program do you—"

"Hey, whoa, slow down," he said, chuckling, silently warning himself not to get too excited about her excitement. She was like a child with a new toy, that's all. It didn't mean any more than that. He'd be crazy to think it did. But he began answering her questions, anyway.

"And that's my latest acquisition," he said finally, pointing her toward a corral set off by itself. A dappled gray yearling colt trotted up to the fence as they came up to it. "This is Hi," he said, reaching out to scratch the young stallion's velvety muzzle. "Yahiya ibn Abdu," he added, giving the animal's official "paper" name. "He's going to father a lot of prizewinners when he's a little older."

"Why, he looks just like Ali," Victoria said, climbing up on the lowest rung of the fence for a better look. "Ali's a little darker now. Down the middle of his back and on his legs, especially. But he was almost this color when he was younger. And he has the exact same shading on his face." She studied the animal for a moment, rubbing her palm on his wide forehead between his soft liquid-black eyes. "His eyes are a tad wider set, I think. What did you say his name was? Yahiya ibn Abdu?"

John nodded.

"Sired by Morgan Breckle's Royal Abdu from Las Vegas, right?"

"Yeah," he said slowly, respect showing in his eyes. She knew a lot more about horses than he'd given her credit for. It took a sharp eye to notice the subtle distinctions between one horse and another, and more than a fleeting interest in breeding to be able to connect those horses to each other by a name. Not to mention knowing the name of the breeder. The little lady, he thought, was full of surprises. Unsettling surprises.

"So was Ali!" she said with a pleased smile. Another link had been forged between them. "Out of Fatima." She patted the colt again, approvingly. "Who was his dame?"

"One of my own mares. Gray Pigeon."

"Well, he's beautiful," she sighed, giving him one more caress before jumping down from the fence. "Your whole herd is beautiful." She lifted her arm, her gesture encompassing all the horses in all the corrals. "Can I see the barn now?"

"I thought you wanted to see the house," he said quickly. He couldn't take her into the barn. The barn was dark and quiet and secluded. There were empty horse stalls in the barn, filled with sweet straw. Striped horse blankets were all too conveniently placed. And sunlight poured in through the open haydoors under the peaked roof. It spilled down between the heavy crossbeam supports in the ceiling, casting bars of light over the stalls at the back of the building, catching dustmotes in its buttery, golden light so that they looked like fireflies dancing through the still, quiet air.

He knew exactly how they looked because he'd stood there, just two days ago, staring at them transfixed, his mind off imagining what they would look like dancing over Victoria Dillon's bare honeyed skin as she lay naked on a horse blanket in one of those stalls. The fantasy had been so real that he'd actually thought he heard her soft moans of need and the strangled sigh of com-

pletion he knew she'd give when her climax came. And
then he'd set his teeth and yanked his mind out of its
playpen and gathered up the camping gear he'd come
to get.

If he took her into the barn now, he'd be all too
tempted to take her, period. And he wasn't going to do
that. He might never be able to let her go if he did. She
wasn't the woman for him, not by a long shot.

"Just keep telling yourself that, Redcloud," he muttered to himself.

"I'm sorry?" Victoria said. "What did you say?"

"One of the mares in there is only a couple of weeks
away from foaling," he said, steering her away from the
barn. "Strangers make her nervous. Let's go up to the
house."

"Fine," said Victoria, willingly falling into step beside him. She was intensely curious about the inside of
his house. What would it tell her about him? About his
life? How much Anglo influence would there be? How
much Navajo?

They walked across the planked deck silently, both
of them caught up in their own feelings. John was wary
about exposing yet another corner of his life to her unsettling, unsuitable influence, yet almost boyishly eager to show her his home. Victoria simmered with
curiosity and a strange kind of excitement. Both of
them were poised on the edge of something they
couldn't quite define. Passion about to be unleashed,
perhaps. Commitments about to be made. Knowledge
to be gained. This was a turning point. Instinctively
they both knew that.

The brass knob turned under his hand, the heavy oak
door opening inward under the pressure of his palm.

Almost holding her breath, Victoria stepped onto the large Mexican tiles of the entryway.

The first thing she noticed was the coolness, the kind of coolness that came from an air conditioner humming efficiently off in some corner of the house. That was definitely Anglo. The next thing she noticed was the magnificent rendering of a sandpainting on one whole wall of the living room. Definitely Navajo.

"That's from the Blessing Way ceremony," he said, noticing where she was looking. "It's usually given to ensure good luck or to celebrate a happy event. Nina and Bob will have Blessing Way songs at their wedding, 'for good hope.' I thought it was an appropriate symbol when I built this place."

"It's beautiful." She stepped down the two wide, shallow, tiled steps onto the bare wooden floor of the living room to get a closer look. "Did you paint it?"

"My father did. He was in training to be a Singer when he was younger. But he gave it up after the divorce."

"Singer?" Victoria said over her shoulder.

"What you Anglos would call a medicine man," he explained, watching her look around the sparsely furnished room.

"Does he live here with you?"

"He died six years ago. Cirrhosis of the liver."

Victoria turned from the painting. "Oh, John. I'm sorry." Those few words explained a lot. His wariness of her was more than just because he'd had an Anglo wife who couldn't accept his life on the reservation. His father had had an Anglo wife, too, and that marriage hadn't worked out, either.

"It'd been a long time coming," John said. "He was ready."

"I'm still sorry."

"Thank you," he said simply, and then extended a hand toward an arched doorway to his left. "Would you like to see the rest of the house?" The subject was closed.

"Yes, please." Victoria was content to let it rest, for now. "Is that the kitchen?"

It was. Victoria found the room sparsely but pleasantly decorated with a few pieces of Indian pottery, furnished simply with a long trestle-style table and modern electrical appliances. It would take only a few feminine touches to make it really homey—a collection of cactus plants on the counter, a bowl of flowers on the table, a set of brightly colored food canisters, curtains at the window.

She turned back into the living room for a second, more thorough look. Sand-colored walls provided a soothing background for the desert colors of the furnishings. A fluffy sheepskin rug lay over the back of the sofa. A geometric-patterned Navajo rug in soft sunset shades of orange and red and yellow picked up the reddish cast of the natural stone fireplace and the sienna tiles of the entryway. Again, all it would take would be a few extra pieces—a conveniently placed end table or two, a lamp for reading, shiny brass candlesticks on the mantel—plus a good dusting to take away the unlived-in look to make it a truly comfortable and welcoming room. In her mind's eye Victoria was already busy placing some of her own furniture around the room, adding to and complementing what was already there.

"What's through there?" she asked, eager to see the rest of it. She was learning a lot about John by seeing his house. He was tidy. He had a good sense of color and design, one that dovetailed with her own. And he was lonely. The rooms she had seen shouted his loneliness. He didn't really live in this house, he just occupied it.

"Just the bedrooms and my office. Nothing that would interest you."

"But they do," Victoria said. "Everything about you interests me."

"What kind of thing is that to say?"

"The truth," she said simply. "Can I look?"

He shrugged, unable to fathom her reasons but unwilling to deny her what she wanted. "Be my guest."

The first room was his office. Filled bookcases lined two walls. A "white" board with some kind of complicated computer flowchart scrawled on it in blue and red marking pens took up most of a third. A three-drawer file cabinet and a copier shared the fourth wall. Most of the center of the room was occupied by a large, rectangular, desk-height table. It held two computer terminals, one of them with its screen blinking, silently talking to another computer through the modem connecting it to one of the two telephones, two printers and several stacks of computer paper, technical journals and school textbooks. A half-full coffee cup sat on top of one of the stacks of paper, an empty bowl of what once might have been beef stew sat on the floor beside his chair. This was where he lived when he was here, she thought. This was where he buried himself in his work and forgot the loneliness of the rest of the house.

"Looks like control central," Victoria said lightly, turning down the hall again.

The next two rooms were presumably meant to be bedrooms; they were empty. The last room was his. A king-size bed set against the longest wall, covered with a huge, spectacular Navajo blanket that would have sold for a couple of thousand dollars in her father's department store. A natural-stone fireplace occupied the entire north wall. Sliding glass doors, draped with loosely woven fabric that matched the bedspread, led out to the deck. A chest of drawers stood opposite. And that was it.

He'd built this house, or had it built, for the Anglo wife who hadn't wanted it. The Navajo bedspread had been a wedding present, undoubtedly from his grandmother, just as the sandpainting on the living room wall had been a gift from his father. And his wife hadn't wanted it, wouldn't even give it a chance.

Stupid, stupid woman, Victoria thought, sadness and anger and an intense gladness warring for dominance in her heart. Sadness for the hurt John must have felt; anger at the woman who had made him feel it; gladness that that woman had never lived here with him.

Because *she* was going to live here with him. *She* was going to be the woman who taught him that not all Anglos were selfish and spoiled. *She* was going to be the woman to banish the loneliness and fill this house with warmth and laughter and love and the children so obviously intended to occupy those empty bedrooms. She turned to tell him so and found him standing right behind her.

"It's a beautiful home, John," she said, looking up at him with her heart in her eyes.

Those spitfire eyes, he thought, *burning with passion, soft and glowing as embers, everything, all at once.*

"I'm glad you like it."

"I do." She put her hand on his chest. "I like it very much."

His heart started to thud into her palm. "Victoria." Somehow his hands were on her shoulders, cupping the fragile bones. "Victoria."

"Yes?"

He groaned and pulled her to him. "Damn," he said softly, lowering his mouth to hers. "Damn. I promised myself I wouldn't do this."

11

"OH, VICTORIA," HE SAID again a moment later, lifting his mouth from hers only far enough to see into her eyes. "I didn't mean for this to happen."

"I know."

"I fought it."

"I know."

"But, dammit, I want you." His lips moved against her mouth as he spoke. His hands flexed against her shoulders. "From the moment I pulled up behind your car on the highway, I've wanted you. I can't sleep. I can't eat. I look at you and see you wanting me back, and I—"

"I *know*," she said, sliding her hand up his shirtfront to curl around the back of his neck. She pulled his head down to hers. "Kiss me."

He kissed her. Hungrily. Passionately. As if he would never get enough. His tongue invaded her mouth, delving into the hot sweetness beyond the barrier of her lips, tasting her. His big, hard hands caressed her back through the silky stuff of her T-shirt, molding her to him, then dropped lower, curving over the swell of her buttocks in the rumpled shorts. His fingertips just touched the soft skin at the top of her thighs, and he lifted her to his body, pressing her hips against the aching hardness of his arousal.

Victoria moaned in helpless delight and melted against him, boneless as a rag doll. Her arms tightened around his neck, pulling him closer. Her lips closed around his tongue, sucking. Her fragrance surrounded him, intensified by the scalding heat of their bodies.

Night-blooming flowers and forbidden sex; the thought broke through the frenzied rapture that clouded his brain. Only she wasn't forbidden now. She was his. In this instant, this mindless moment out of time, she was his. Every hot, silky, responsive inch of her, yearning for him as passionately as he yearned for her.

He slid his hand up her side and ran the heel of his hand over the swell of her breast.

"Yes," she sighed into his mouth, turning her body to give him fuller access.

He took it, sliding his hand inward to completely cover her breast. It was as soft, as sweet, as delicate as he had known it would be. The nipple was a hard little pebble, pressing insistently against the sensitive center of his palm through the layers of her clothes.

He had to have her naked. Now. He had to see what he'd only dreamed about for what seemed like weeks. Months. Years. "Victoria," he whispered, easing her away from him with his hands on her hips.

She resisted at first, reaching blindly to pull his mouth back to hers. Delicious mouth. Talented mouth. Sexy, sensitive mouth. She wanted to go on kissing him forever.

"Victoria." His voice was a whisper of woodsmoke. "Victoria, let me undress you."

"Oh, yes." Her hands fell to the belt at her waist. "Yes. I want to be naked with you."

He reached to stop her. "Let *me* undress you," he said, brushing her eager hands out of the way.

"Oh." Her hands dropped to her sides. "All right," she said docilely, trusting herself to his ministrations.

"I've dreamed of undressing you," he said softly, unbuckling her belt. "Daydreams, night dreams. The thought was always there." He flicked open the waistband button. "Every time I looked at you I wanted to do this." He lowered the zipper.

Victoria's throat worked as she swallowed. Her eyes closed.

"From that first day, when your skirt came up— Remember?"

Victoria nodded, her breathing shallow and fast.

"And I got that tantalizing little glimpse of that scrap of lace you call underpants—" He slid his hands inside the parted cloth. Lace brushed his palms as they skimmed across her belly to her hips. He sucked in his breath with a hiss and pushed the baggy shorts away. They fell, unimpeded, down the long silky length of her legs to pool around her ankles. He followed them down with his hands, his palms outlining the curves of her thighs and calves, cupping her heels to pull off her tennis shoes as she lifted each foot out of the shorts.

He straightened, running his hands back up the same way, his fingers whispering frantically up over the curves of her body to grasp the hem of her T-shirt. He pulled it off over her head in a single swift motion. Victoria raised her arms like an obedient child, then dropped them back to her sides, waiting. Her hair, ruffled by the T-shirt, settled softly back on her shoulders.

The honey-colored stretch-lace teddy she was wearing underneath fitted her like a second skin. The legs were high cut, revealing the smooth curve of her hips all the way to her waist. The low U-necked bodice, held up by two narrow lace bands over her shoulders, molded itself to the shape of her breasts. He could see the outline of her nipples and the soft black shadow of the hair between her thighs.

This little scrap of nothing, this invitation to ecstasy, was what she'd been wearing that night he'd stood in the trees and watched her shadow on the tent. No wonder he'd thought she was naked under her jeans.

"Lord, Victoria," he groaned, his big hands reaching for her again. "Why do you even bother?" His mouth covered hers before she could answer.

It didn't matter. He knew why she bothered. It was all a plot to drive him stark raving crazy. And it was working. He was mad with wanting her.

He bent without removing his mouth from hers and lifted her in his arms. Victoria gave a satisfied sigh and tightened her arms around his neck. By feel alone, he made his way over to the bed, stopping when he felt it come up against his knees. He lifted his knee to the mattress and leaned over, lowering her to the striped Navajo blanket. Their mouths finally separated, then, her arms falling away as he drew back and looked down at her with his hands braced on either side of her supine body.

She looked so damned *right*, he thought almost despairingly, lying there on his bed with her silky ebony hair spread out against the deep blues and greens of the blanket his grandmother had made for him. Sunlight filtered through the loosely woven drapes at the window, dappling her warm, golden-honey skin, gilding her high, elegant cheekbones, shimmering over the moisture his kisses had left on her ruby lips. If he forgot about where she came from, about her pampered life outside the reservation, it would be easy to believe that she was Indian herself. To believe that she could belong here.

She smiled up at him softly, sweetly, her brown eyes glowing like the embers of a fire. "What is it?" she whispered, raising her hand to touch his cheek. "Why have you stopped?"

He turned his lips into her palm. "I haven't stopped," he told her. "I was just taking a minute to look, that's all."

Her smile deepened. "I'd like to look, too, you know."

"You would, would you?"

"Um-hmm." Her hand slipped down his cheek and throat, inside the collar of his shirt, to the first pearl-headed snap. A gentle tug had it open. The small charm around his neck swung forward on its short leather thong. "I've had a few fantasies of my own about what you look like under your clothes, too." She tugged the second snap open, then came upright on the bed, pushing him back so that he sat on its edge, facing her. She knelt in front him, using both hands to finish unsnapping his shirt. "That very first day, when you stopped to help me and came strutting up to my car with—"

"Strutting!"

"Strutting up to my car," she said positively, pulling the shirttails out of his waistband, "with your shirt hanging open and your chest all hard and gleaming with sweat. I kept hoping you'd take your shirt completely off so I could get a better look at all that virile beauty."

"Well, now," he drawled, embarrassed. "Is that any way for a little lady to talk?"

Victoria gave him a playful, narrowed-eyed glare. "That's the way this little lady talks," she informed him, mock tough. "Any objections?"

"No, none at all, ma'am." He grinned. "Go right on ahead talking any way you want to."

"Thank you," she said seriously. "Now, where was I?"

"Wanting me to take my shirt off so you could get a better look."

"I didn't want to just look. I wanted to touch you, too . . . Rub my hands all over your chest to see if all those gorgeous muscles you were flexing at me were as hard as they looked." She parted the edges of his shirt and smoothed her palms over him. A satisfied purr rumbled in her throat. "They are."

"There's another part of my anatomy that's pretty hard right now," he said.

"Yeah?" Head tilted, she gave him a flirtatious, seductive look from under half-lowered lashes and trailed her fingers down the center of his muscled torso to his turquoise belt buckle. "Would it help if I rubbed it, too?"

"Victoria!" He pressed a hand over her teasing fingers, flattening them against his stomach before they could curl around his hardness.

"John!" she said back, mimicking the half-shocked tone of his voice. She giggled. "I'd've never thought you'd turn out to be such a prude," she teased.

"Prude?" he said incredulously. *"Prude!"* He stood. "I'll show you prude, little lady," he threatened, shrugging out of his shirt. He dropped it to the floor with careless disregard and reached for the buckle on his belt. The tongue slithered through the first loop. He bent it back, unfastening the buckle, then pushed the two ends aside with his wrists and pulled open the metal buttons on his fly. They popped apart easily, helped, no doubt, she thought, by the hard bulge pressing against them from the other side.

"Take it off," sang Victoria from the bed in a strangled little voice. "Take it all off."

John stopped undressing, his hands on the waistband of his jeans, and scowled at her. "This isn't the way you acted in my fantasies," he accused.

"No?" She came up on her knees suddenly and reached out, wrapping her arms around his lean hips. She pressed her cheek to his stomach, her chest to his hips. "Is this better?" she whispered fiercely.

"It'll—" John paused and cleared his throat. "It'll do for a start." He cupped the back of her head with his hand, stroking the raven hair, then curled his hand around her nape, urging her to look up at him. "Victoria," he murmured, tenderness welling up in him from out of nowhere.

She lifted her head. Their eyes met and held for an endless second, all teasing fading with that long, longing look.

"Victoria," John said again, sinking down onto the bed with her in his arms. He touched her face with wondering fingertips, tracing the high cheekbones, the straight little nose, the delicate jaw, the chin that could look so irresistibly arrogant. She lifted it now, offering her throat for his delectation. He buried his lips against the pulse beating just above her collarbone, his hand skimming down the fragile bones of her chest to cup her breast.

Victoria moaned softly, approvingly, and reached out to touch him in turn, yearning to feel the hard, smooth muscles of his arms and shoulders and chest under her questing fingers.

So smooth, she thought, caressing him as he caressed her. *So warm. So wonderful.* Was any other man so perfectly made? So precisely what he should be? So exactly what she needed him to be in both body and spirit?

She felt languid, all liquid and warm, as they lay there together in the quiet room; as if she could stay there with him forever, exactly as they were now, kissing and touching and murmuring soft, unintelligible words into each other's mouths, floating on the sweet feeling that wrapped around them like a cloud.

But the feeling became gradually hotter, the kisses deeper, the caresses bolder, the words more raw and needy until, suddenly, John was looming over her, naked, his big hands tugging at the lace straps on her shoulders. Victoria lifted her body—her shoulders, her torso, her hips, her legs each in turn—assisting him as he peeled her out of the teddy.

Her body was more perfect than any fantasy could ever possibly be. He had envisioned her naked, yes. He'd been able to picture the narrow, boyish hips, the tiny waist that had felt so small in his hands, the delicate rib cage, the soft swell of her breasts. But it hadn't occurred to him that the honey-gold color of her silky skin owed nothing to the kiss of the sun. He hadn't imagined that her nipples and the surrounding aureoles would be the same deep rose as her lips. He hadn't realized that the tangle of black curls at the apex of her thighs would be the softest thing he had ever touched. He reached down, his callused fingers skimming over her soft stomach, to cup that feminine delta.

They both sighed.

And then his fingers began to move, seeking even softer, creamier flesh, gently stroking the little nub hidden there, and Victoria's sighs turned to moans. The moans turned to whimpers. And the whimpers turned, finally, to a muffled scream of fulfillment. Almost before she had her breath back, he was moving over her, parting her thighs with his knees, positioning himself for entry.

"Victoria," he moaned, sinking into her warm, welcoming moistness.

As if she knew exactly what he wanted, exactly what he needed, she lifted her legs and locked her ankles behind his hips. Matching him thrust for thrust, heartbeat for heartbeat, breath for ragged breath, she held his strong, trembling body in her arms and poured out her love in silent waves of feeling.

"Oh, John," she moaned when her second climax took her. "John, my love. My love," she sighed when passion finally claimed him, driving his body into hers with one last mighty thrust.

JOHN HAD HEARD HER whispered endearment; just as he had heard every moan and sigh and soft murmur she had uttered before that. He told himself that it meant nothing. It was only a word spoken in the throes of passion. She probably hadn't even realized she'd said it. So how could she have meant it?

The terrifying thing was that he wanted her to mean it. He wanted her to open her chocolate eyes and look up into his with the same soft, sweet expression she'd given him the other night outside her tent, and say it again. And he wanted her to mean it. Even if she lied.

Because it would be a lie. If not now, then soon. She wasn't the kind of woman who could call a man like him "my love" forever. Sooner or later reality would intrude. And reality was the hardship and harshness of life on an Indian reservation. Reality was the inability of someone like her, someone non-Indian, someone pampered and spoiled and used to all the advantages of "civilization" to endure the harshness he'd chosen for any length of time. It wasn't her fault. It wasn't his. It just was. And he was a fool for wishing it were different, for wishing that this interlude could be more than what it was.

But still he wished.

"John?" Victoria's soft voice broke into his thoughts. Her hand stroked gently through the damp hair on his forehead. "John, have you fallen asleep on me?"

He raised his head. Her eyes were soft and content, glowing like banked embers. Just as he had imagined they would be after loving. "Would I be that impolite?" he asked, smiling at her.

"Probably," she said, smiling back. "But I wouldn't mind. I just thought maybe you could shift over a tad so I can breathe. I might take a little nap myself then."

He levered himself off her, rolling to his side, and cradled her in one arm. "Better?"

She snuggled her cheek into his shoulder and put her hand on his chest. "Perfect," she said. But she lied.

Oh, physically everything was perfect. It had never been more perfect. Emotionally she was feeling a little shaky. Where were the words of love? Or the endearments, at least, if he wasn't quite ready to say the big *L* word yet?

She could understand that he wasn't. Two important women in his life had been "women like her," on the surface at least, and they had let him down. Hurt him badly. She could see that he might not be quite ready to risk that hurt again, especially with a woman who hadn't yet managed to convince him that she was more than willing—that she was eager—to live life his way. But did that mean she wasn't going to get any sweet nothings at all?

"You have the softest, silkiest skin," he said then, brushing his fingers down her spine. She felt his face press against the top of her head, heard him inhale deeply. "And you smell so damned sexy."

Victoria's heart turned over, her touch of postcoital sadness disappearing at the sound of his woodsmoke voice.

"What do you call that perfume you wear?"

Victoria shifted in his embrace, coming up on her left elbow to look down at him. She placed her right arm across his chest and propped her chin on the back of her hand. "It's called Victoria. I have it specially blended just for me."

"That figures," he snorted, smiling up at her lazily. Maybe she wasn't a woman for forever, he thought—a woman who had perfume made to order certainly didn't belong on the reservation—but she was here now. He would deal with her being gone when she was gone. "What's in it?"

"Tuberose and musk, mostly. With a touch of sandalwood."

"Well, I like it."

"I'll wear it for you always," she promised, moving her hand to kiss his chest lightly. He smiled again, and she inched up and over him, scattering soft little baby kisses over his smooth flesh. Her lips touched the charm around his neck. She nudged it with her index finger. "Does this have some special significance?"

"Not really," John hedged.

"But it's a Zuni fetish, isn't it? Although—" she rolled it over his chest with her finger "—from what I've read, most fetishes are animals of some kind, for good luck in hunting or whatever. This looks like a human figure."

"Changing Woman," John said.

"Changing Woman?"

"She's the major female god-figure in Navajo mythology."

"I know who she is," Victoria interrupted. "But why are you wearing her around your neck?"

"To protect me from women like you."

"What?" Victoria pushed herself upright by his side.

John found himself smiling at the outraged look on her face. "My grandmother had it made when I came back to the reservation after my divorce. It's not exactly orthodox, but basically her reasoning was that since Changing Woman is the premier Navajo female figure, wearing her image should protect me from unsuitable Anglo floozies like you."

Victoria grinned, a deliciously wicked, seductively feminine grin. "Didn't work very well, did it?" she said, and stretched out on top of him.

THEY MADE LOVE AGAIN, then stripped back the bedspread and slept and woke only to make love a third time. Each time, they revealed a little more of themselves, a little more of what made them uniquely them.

"I married right after college," Victoria said at one point as she lay, lazy and contented, in John's arms. "Brad was 'perfect' for me. The right age, the right background, the right family. He was a merchandising major, and he took a position at the store after our wedding. Not because he married me," she assured John. "He'd have gotten the job, anyway. He's still there, in fact. But it was another thing that made us so 'perfect' together."

"Did you love him?"

"I thought I did." She placed a sleepy kiss on John's shoulder. "But that was before I knew better."

"I'VE HAD THIS ONE recurring fantasy," John confessed in a hoarse whisper, his thumbs stroking back and forth over her turgid nipples as she rocked above him.

"Which is?" Victoria prompted breathlessly, looking down at him through lambent, half-closed eyes.

"You'd be astride me just...oh that's so good!...just like you are now, except . . . except, ah, Victoria!"

"Except what?" she panted.

"Except that you'd have all your clothes on."

"All my clothes?"

"Not . . . not your panties. You'd have taken them off already and— Yes, just like that." He put his hands on her hips, urging her on, helping her to quicken the pace.

"And?"

"And I'd still have my jeans on, but . . . but opened, of course. We'd be parked on the side of the road in the truck and couldn't get completely undr—"

"In the truck?" Victoria said, laughter and passion in her voice. Her breathing was becoming more and more labored. "You . . . you too?"

"Me too?"

"I had a fantasy about the truck."

"You did?" He dropped his hand to the place where their bodies joined and found her with his thumb. "Did I do this in your fantasy?"

"IT'S NOT THAT MY MOTHER didn't try," John said, absently stroking Victoria's ebony hair as he spoke. "She did. For seven years she gave it her best shot. But in the end, she just couldn't take it. And she was worried about me, too," he said, wanting to show her all sides of it. "She wanted me to have a good education, and she didn't think I'd get it on the reservation. And then there was my dad's drinking."

She felt him move against the pillows, shifting into a more comfortable position, as if the words he spoke had made him uncomfortable.

"It got to be a big problem toward the end. He'd take to the bottle because he felt her pulling away, and she'd pull further away because of the drinking."

"I'm sorry," Victoria said, her eyes clouding at the thought of the little boy who'd seen his parent's marriage slowly fall apart.

"Oh, it wasn't all that bad for me," John denied. "That's one of the advantages of living in an extended family. There was always someone there to take up the slack or soften the blow. I didn't really know what had gone on until years later."

Victoria understood what he was saying, but she couldn't help wishing that he'd never had to feel the blow at all.

"Anyway, Mom remarried when I was eleven. She and her husband still live in Flagstaff."

"Do you see her often?"

"Sure. I get to Flagstaff four or five times a year. Most of the companies I do business with are in Flagstaff."

"Companies you do business with?"

"I design software systems."

"Oh, yes," Victoria said, remembering his office. "Control central."

"OH, VICTORIA," JOHN GROANED, tangling his hands in her hair. "You never did *that* in any of my fantasies."

She lifted her head for a moment. "Do you want me to stop?" Her voice was husky, thick with the wonder of loving him, intoxicated with the power she was discovering she had over his big body.

"No . . . God, no. . . ."

THEY WERE IN HIS KITCHEN. Victoria stood at the stove in one of John's shirts, stirring soup. John sat at one end of the trestle table, wearing jeans and nothing else, carefully spreading Skippy peanut butter and Smucker's blackberry jam on bread. They had missed lunch.

"I have a teaching degree," Victoria was saying, "but I haven't ever taught school."

"Because you got married right after college?"

"Mostly. Brad didn't see any reason for me to work and, since I didn't have a burning desire to influence young minds, I didn't disagree. But lately—" *Very lately.* "Well, lately I've been seriously thinking of looking into getting a teaching position. Maybe—" she licked her lips and stared down into the soup "—maybe here on the reservation."

John was silent for a moment, wrestling down the surge of joy her statement brought. If she taught on the reservation, then they could— But, no, he'd seen plenty of bored young Anglos come to the reservation for a semester or two, even a year or two, burning to bring education and culture to the Red Man. Some of them were actually dedicated to what they were doing. Very few of them ever stayed. She wouldn't stay, either. Not more than a month, tops.

"I would've thought some classy, private girls' school would have been more your cup of tea," he said mildly.

"They don't need me at some classy girls' school." *You need me.* "Nina said there's always a need for good teachers on the reservation."

"And you, with all your experience, are a good teacher?"

"I could be," she said, stung. She stirred the soup harder, biting her lip to keep the tears from overflowing.

John stopped spreading peanut butter on the sandwiches and stood up. She looked so damned dejected all of a sudden, with her shoulders hunched up as if he'd hit her. He hadn't meant to hurt. He'd only meant to be the voice of reason. She would probably be a good teacher. Hell, an excellent teacher. She had the knack of relating to kids on their level; Christina thought she was wonderful. But she belonged in some fancy, well-equipped city school, not here.

He put his hand on her shoulder and turned her around. "Victoria, I'm sorry. I didn't mean that the way it sounded."

"Yes, you did," she accused him. "You meant it exactly the way it sounded. But you're wrong. I'd be a great teacher. And I'd be a great teacher right here on the reservation."

He shook his head. "This isn't the place for you."

"Yes, it is," she said evenly. "This is exactly the place for me. Mostly..." It was unexpectedly hard to say; she'd never had to admit to loving someone who hadn't already admitted to loving her first. "Mostly because you're here. And I want to be where you are but—"

"Victoria, don't say—"

"But I'd want to stay here, anyway," she went on firmly, "even if I weren't in love with you, because I can make a difference here. I can be useful."

"You're not in love with me, Victoria," John said desperately, trying to make himself believe his own words. She couldn't be in love with him, because— dammit all to hell!—he couldn't be in love with her. He wouldn't let himself be. "It's lust. That's all. Just lust."

"You don't feel anything else for me? Nothing at all?"

"Affection," John said reluctantly. "A great deal of liking. That's all you feel, too."

"That's *not* all I feel," she said stubbornly, her chin up. "I'm in love with you, John Redcloud. And there's not a damned thing you can do about it. So you're just going to have to learn to live with it."

12

HE AVOIDED HER for the next two days. Two days in which Victoria was busier and worked harder than she ever had in her life. Maria seemed suddenly intent on "learning her soul" in the shortest time possible— through the simple but effective expedient of working her to death. Or it might just have been, Victoria reflected wryly, that with all there was to do in preparation for the wedding, Maria Redcloud had forgotten Victoria's soul altogether and was simply taking advantage of every available pair of hands. Whatever the reason, Victoria found herself harvesting vegetables, hauling water and grinding corn—by hand—as if she'd been doing these things all her life.

It was tiring, working so hard at unfamiliar tasks, but satisfying, too, to see the results of her labor, to know that what she did with her own two hands was of real value to real people. And she knew that, given time and experience, the tasks would become more familiar, less tiring and even more enjoyable.

Well, most of them would. She opted out of watching Matt Redcloud slaughter Christina's sheep, electing to stay at the *ramada* when the child urged her to come and see the sheep prepared for the wedding feast.

"Grandmother's going to help me cure the hide," Christina said, hoping to entice Victoria to join her with that added inducement.

Victoria just shook her head and kept grinding corn in the wide, shallow stone bowl that had been used to grind corn for generations. Nothing, not even Maria Redcloud's pointed look as she left the *ramada*, was going to budge her from the shelter while some poor dumb sheep was being "prepared" for dinner. Even John, if he'd been there, couldn't have persuaded her to participate.

She was glad, though, that he wasn't around to see her squeamishness. Undoubtedly he would feel that a woman who really belonged here would be able to slaughter a sheep every day before breakfast and slap it on the fire without ever turning a hair. She, on the other hand, would rather not have to look at her dinner until after it had ceased to resemble the animal it came from. John would take that as just another example of her pampered life-style, another reason why she wouldn't last a month.

She noted, though, that he wasn't around to volunteer to help with getting the lamb chops from their natural state to the table. But, then neither did Nina.

"No, thank you, Christina," the bride-to-be said in answer to the child's invitation to come watch. "I have to finish this last bit of beadwork." She indicated the tunic in her lap. Victoria knew the last bead had been sewn on ten minutes ago; Nina had just been sitting there, admiring it with a dreamy look on her face. "Weak stomach," she confessed in answer to Victoria's questioning look after Christina had gone. "Unlike that bloodthirsty little monster," she said affectionately, "I prefer to think that all my meat comes wrapped in plastic." She grinned. "Thank God, most of it does."

"Huh?" Victoria said.

"Don't let Grandmother fool you," Nina said, immediately understanding Victoria's inarticulate question. "She lives 'as the Navajo have always lived' only in the summer," she said, carefully folding her tunic so that the intricate beadwork wouldn't catch on itself. "All this—the hogans, the cook fire, the outdoor plumbing—is only when the Redcloud clan comes to the canyon. And there are many Redclouds who never come to the canyon at all, except for special family occasions like the wedding. Or Redclouds like myself and John who go back and forth, like—" she paused, looking for a word "—like commuters in the city," she said, obviously pleased with the analogy. "But in the wintertime even Grandmother lives in town. She makes her home in Chinle with my mother and father, in a house with running water and electricity and a color television set." She smoothed a hand over the soft suede, then looked up and smiled. "Her favorite program is *Dallas*."

"You're kidding," Victoria said, unable to picture Maria Redcloud in a house, let alone sitting in front of a television set. "Really?"

"Really," Nina assured her. "And if it weren't for the wedding tomorrow, most of the work that's been going on around here wouldn't be, either."

Victoria nodded. She'd realized that herself; there was no way the Redcloud family, as large as it was, could eat all the food she'd helped gather and chop and cook over the past two days.

"You certainly wouldn't be doing any of that," Nina said, a nod of her dark head indicating the corn that Victoria was grinding. "It's for the traditional cornmeal mush that Bob and I will eat during the wedding ceremony—and for corn pudding that Christina likes so much, of course. But if it weren't for the wedding, Grandmother would have made the pudding with packaged cornmeal from the supermarket. Although," Nina mused thoughtfully, "I'm a little surprised that she set you to grinding it. Not that you aren't doing a perfectly fine job," she added quickly, making amends for what might have sounded like an insult. "It's just that it's a little unusual that she'd trust a virtual stranger with such a traditional task."

But Victoria hadn't taken any insult; she hadn't even heard the last part of what Nina had said. "The Navajo have always been adept at picking and choosing those aspects of an alien culture that suit their needs and ignoring what doesn't," she said softly, her hands pausing in their task as she stared off into the distance.

"Yes. That's it exactly," Nina agreed. "How did you know?"

Victoria brought her attention back to the corn. "I read it somewhere."

"Well, it's Grandmother to a T," Nina said, getting up to fold her wedding tunic away for one more day's safekeeping.

It was John to a T, too, thought Victoria. He picked and chose among the traditions of his two heritages, finding and using what suited him, discarding what didn't—from both cultures. He might wear a Zuni fetish around his neck, she thought, and have his own hogan on his grandmother's ancestral land in the Canyon de Chelly. He might raise horses like generations of Navajo men before him and have a Blessing Way sandpainting on his wall. But he didn't really believe in the power of the fetish, and he used the hogan, not as his home, but like an Anglo might use a summer fishing cabin in the mountains. The horses he raised were blooded Arabians, not mustangs raided from his Apache neighbors. And the Blessing Way sandpainting was painted on a wall in a house that any hardworking, Anglo rancher would be proud to call his own.

And furthermore, she thought, pounding furiously, that ranch house was filled with more modern computer equipment than any normal, run-of-the-mill rancher—Anglo, Navajo or Mexican grandee—was ever likely to see, let alone understand. And his cupboards were stocked with Skippy peanut butter, Smucker's jams and Campbell soup, not jerky and dried corn.

John Redcloud, she decided, had picked and chosen until he'd achieved the best of both worlds. Modern Anglo technology for convenience and livelihood, ancient Navajo tradition and service to his people to soothe his soul. And he dared talk to her about being spoiled!

Well, Victoria thought, the cornmeal turning to dust under her stone pestle, *I'll certainly have a few choice words to say to him when he finally shows his face around here!*

HE SHOWED HIS FACE the next day. He had to—it was Nina's wedding day. He arrived during the lull after breakfast had been eaten and cleared away and everyone was taking a breather before they had to begin preparations for the wedding.

Christina's sheep, looking more like a main dish than an animal now, was spitted over the embers of a slow-burning fire, roasting to a tender turn. Huge pots of garden-fresh beans, squash casserole and tamale pie were being kept warm in round brick ovens. Corn tortillas and loaves of fresh-baked bread waited for last-minute heating. Cakes and pies snuggled safely in covered baskets. Store-bought relishes, olives and pickles waited to be opened. The corn pudding had been made. The ceremonial corn mush simmered on the camp stove.

The bride was in her mother's hogan, attended by her mother and sister, taking a ritual bath in yucca suds before being dressed for her wedding. Maria was poking the cook fires. The men of the family were gathered under the *ramada*, engaged in a low-voiced discussion. Ricky and Christina were squatting in the dust, playing a game of cat's cradle. Victoria sat on a flat rock in the sun, watching them and wondering how she might get back to the lodge to change into a dress for the wedding. Wondering, too, when John was finally going to show up so she could give him a piece of her mind.

"John, John!" Christina said suddenly, abandoning the game she was playing with her brother. "Do you see my sheep being cooked?" she shouted, running up to him to hang on his leg.

"I smell it," he said, licking his lips. He reached down to caress her hair. "Smells great."

"I gathered the wood for the fire," Ricky said, unwilling to be left out. "And I helped with the butchering." He gave his sister a smug look. "Christina only watched. It was neat, John," he said with the ghoulishness particular to little boys everywhere. "Grandfather cut the—"

"I've seen it done before," John interrupted. He'd seen it done but he didn't like it. Weak stomach.

"We have missed you these past two days," Maria said in Navajo as he walked toward the cook fire with a child on each side. "Where have you been?"

"Thinking," John said in English.

"You are troubled?" Maria asked, with a quick look at Victoria. "You are unsure in your mind about something?"

"No, nothing," he lied, glancing over to where Victoria was sitting with the sun shining on her hair.

She looked back at him with a particularly martial light in her chocolate eyes.

He shifted uneasily, sensing . . . something. Trouble, he thought, though what trouble she could cause him that she hadn't already, he didn't know.

"I'm glad you're here, John," she said, rising from her seat on the rock. Her chin was in the air.

Definitely trouble.

"I want to talk to your grandmother. We have business to discuss."

"Business?" he said. "With Grandmother?" Why the hell would she want to talk business with his grandmother? She knew all the nonsense about "knowing her soul" was just that—nonsense. So what was the point?

"Yes, business," Victoria said firmly. "With your grandmother. I'd like you to translate for me, please."

"What does she say?" Maria demanded in Navajo.

"You know very well what she says," John said in the same language. "Why don't you just talk to her yourself?"

Maria snorted and waved her hand dismissively.

"Did you tell her what I said?" Victoria asked.

"You haven't said anything yet."

"Well, tell her—" She took a deep breath. "Tell her that I know that she doesn't approve of me. And tell her I know why. Because she knows you're attracted to me. And because she's afraid you'll get hurt."

"What?"

"Tell her," Victoria demanded.

John shrugged. "You heard her," he said to his grandmother in Navajo.

Victoria waited for him to translate the rest. "Is that it?" she said when he didn't.

"That's it. Navajos say a lot with a few words." He looked down at her, trying to steel his heart against her loveliness—and the longing in her eyes. "You finished now?"

"Not by a long shot." She looked Maria square in the eye. "Mrs. Redcloud," she said earnestly, "I know you're worried about your grandson. That he'll fall in love with another Anglo woman and be hurt or leave the reservation. But that won't happen with me. I won't hurt him because—" She stopped, suddenly realizing that she had the undivided attention of every person present. She lifted her chin even higher. "Because I'm in love with him, too."

Too? John thought, fighting panic. *Where'd she get this "too" stuff?* He'd never said the word. He might have felt it, thought it, but he hadn't said it.

"Very much in love with him," she repeated in a clear, strong voice. "And when we're married I want to live here on the reservation with him. I want to teach school here and—"

"Married!" John exploded, aghast at having his greatest fantasy brought out in the open. "Who the hell said anything about marriage? Dammit! It's just lust!" he shouted.

"Marriage?" Maria said in English. "You have asked this young woman to marry you?"

"It's not just lust!" Victoria shouted back, turning on him. "I'm in love with you. Love, not lust. And you're in love with me."

"I never said anything about love!" But he'd thought about it. Oh, yes, he'd thought about it. "And I won't!"

"You don't have to say it. As long as you feel it, that's all I care about," she lied. She wanted desperately to hear him say it. "And I know you feel it, John," she said fiercely, "even if you're too stubborn to admit it."

"Stubborn?" He moved forward a step; they were nearly nose-to-nose. "*You're* calling *me* stubborn?"

"As a jackass!"

"Of all the . . ." Words failed him.

Maria's voice broke between them. "Do you propose to take another bride without consulting me first?" she demanded of her grandson in English, her black eyes shifting between the two combatants.

John's teeth snapped together. "I didn't consult you the first time, Grandmother," he ground out. "I hardly think—"

"No, you did not," Maria agreed with asperity. "And look where it got you."

"Grandmother, please!" John began, then stopped, closed his eyes and took a deep breath, fighting for calm. "You have nothing to worry about, Grandmother," he said then, opening his eyes. Victoria's lovely face filled his vision; he steeled himself against it. "I am *not* going to marry this woman," he said deliberately, staring into her chocolate eyes, struggling to ignore the hurt look that came into them at his words.

"So you say, Grandson. But this woman—" Maria lifted a hand at Victoria "—thinks differently." She pinned her tall, glowering grandson with a censorious look. "What have you done, that she should think this?"

"Done?" John's gaze flickered from Victoria to his grandmother. "I've done nothing!"

A suspicion of a twinkle appeared in Maria's eyes. But just a suspicion. It was gone so fast that John wasn't even sure he'd really seen it. "Nothing?" she said, her black eyes boring into him.

John very nearly blushed. "Nothing," he repeated, trying to convince himself as well as her.

But Maria had already turned away from him. She reached out, took Victoria's chin in her gnarled hand and turned the smooth honey-gold face to her own. She stared intently, her black eyes boring into Victoria's brown ones for endless seconds, looking for God knew what.

Victoria stared back almost defiantly.

"Has my grandson promised you marriage?"

Victoria didn't flinch at the question. "No," she said, not even realizing that they were communicating directly with each other—in English.

"Has he spoken to you of love?"

"Not ex—," she began. Then, "No," she said. "He hasn't *spoken* of it."

"But you have spoken of it to him?"

"Yes." Victoria's eyes went to John's face, then back to Maria's. Her voice was strong and firm. "Yes, I've told John I love him."

Maria nodded, released her chin and reached for her hands. She ran a fingertip over the short, unpolished nails, then turned them over, palms up.

"You have worked hard," she said, touching the small scratches Victoria had earned with four days of work. "You have given a willing hand to whatever was asked of you; you have respected our ways; you have learned your tasks quickly. And you have done all with a joyful spirit." She looked into Victoria's eyes again, then, her look long and searching, her worn, gnarled hands still holding Victoria's smoother ones. Almost as quickly as she'd formed her opinion of the fragile, raven-haired woman, she was changing it.

"You will make your home here, on the reservation?" Maria asked.

"Yes." The word was a mere whisper. "I will make my home here."

"Grandmother—" John began, but Maria silenced him with a gesture.

"You will learn our ways and our customs?" she said to Victoria.

"Yes."

"You will give my grandson children?"

"Yes," Victoria said fervently. "Yes, I will give him children." Triumph blazed in her chocolate eyes for a moment. Maria Redcloud approved of her. "Many children."

Maria patted Victoria's hands, then put them away from her. "You have my blessing on this marriage."

"Now, wait just one goddamned minute!" John exploded. "I haven't heard anyone ask me about all this!"

Victoria turned to him with her heart in her eyes. "Will you marry me, John?"

"Lord, Victoria!" he said, tamping down the surge of joy her words brought him. It wouldn't work. He'd thought about it from every angle over the past two days, and it just wouldn't work. He wouldn't ask her to give up her life. He wouldn't consider giving up his. Which was what it would come to eventually; one of them would lose. "Use your head! We come from two different worlds, and when you get bored with playing Indian you'll go back to yours."

"I'm not playing Indian any more than you are! I love it here. Right here—" she stabbed her finger toward the ground "—in the canyon. And I love it at your ranch. All of it. Everything about it. I...I can't explain it," she added in a low tone, "except to say that for the first time in my life I feel useful. Like I could make a difference. And I love that feeling, John, almost as much as I love you."

"You'll get over it," he said, balling his hands into fists in an effort to keep from reaching for her. "Maybe not next week or next month, but soon. And when you do, you'll leave."

"I won't leave! I want to raise Arabians with you and teach school with you in one of your traveling classrooms." She put her hand on his arm and looked up at him. "I want to have children with you."

"No." He shook her hand off and backed away a step. If she touched him—if she allowed her to touch him— he wouldn't have the strength to do what was best for both of them. "No," he said again, fighting the need to take her in his arms and never let her go. "It won't work. Not in the long run. You'd get sick and tired of life here—of the hardship and harshness of scraping a living out of the desert. And then you'd—"

"Oh, please," she scoffed, advancing on him until they were nose-to-nose again. "You spend three months a year playing summer camp in this beautiful canyon." Her arms opened wide to encompass it. "You have a ranch that any horse breeder, of any culture, would be happy to call his own—not to mention a roomful of computers that NASA wouldn't be ashamed of. You travel to Flagstaff four or five times a year on business. You teach computer science from a traveling van. That doesn't sound like a life of hardship to me," she said forcefully. "It sounds to me like you're living exactly the way you want to, with everything you could possibly want."

John just glared at her, unable to think of anything to say because, he realized suddenly, he *did* have everything he wanted. Or had, until she'd showed up to turn his life upside down. It made him mad as hell. At her. At himself. At the world in general.

"That's right," he said, his voice low and fierce. "I've got everything I want. Everything. I don't need another thing. Especially not a pampered—" he poked his forefinger into her chest "—spoiled rotten—" another poke "—twit like you."

Victoria grabbed his finger in her fist. "Oh, you want me, all right," she returned, equally incensed. "And that's what's—"

"I do not, dammit!" he roared, pulling away from her grasp. "You're not even Navajo!"

Victoria blinked at his seeming non sequitur. "What's that got to do with anything?"

"I swore I'd never marry another woman who wasn't at least part Navajo, that's what it's got to do with it."

"Oh, well . . ." A slow smile spread over Victoria's face. "If that's what all this fuss is about, then there's no problem."

"No problem? No *problem*! Didn't you hear what I just said? The woman I eventually marry won't be some pampered little Anglo with no concept of what life's like on the reservation. She'll be a Navajo, someone who knows and loves this way of life as much as I do."

"No problem," Victoria said again.

John just stared down at her.

"My great-grandmother on my father's side was a Navajo," she said. "My great-grandfather was Conrad Cullen. He had a trading post near Fort Defiance," she continued when he said nothing. "They met when he . . ." She trailed off, realizing suddenly that not only was John staring at her in open-mouthed astonishment, but so was everyone else. "What?" she said, looking around at the circle of faces that surrounded her. "What have I said?"

It was Matt Redcloud who answered her. "Your great-grandmother was Navajo?"

"Yes, of the Bitter-Water clan."

"Why did you not say this before?" Maria demanded.

Victoria shrugged. "It's not something I think about very often. Not anymore than I think about my mother being half French. And, to be totally honest," she said, looking at Maria, "I guess I didn't want you to 'judge my soul' because of who my ancestors are. I wanted you to judge me for myself."

Maria nodded, satisfied with her answer, pleased that, on top of everything else she was, Victoria was part Navajo, too. John was another matter.

"Well, don't think it makes any difference," he warned her, feeling as if he'd been somehow manipulated by the pair of them. "You're still a pampered, spoiled-rotten twit as far as I'm concerned." He turned and stomped off before she could reach out to stop him.

"All right, John Redcloud!" she shouted at his back, incensed. How dare he call *her* spoiled! If ever anyone was spoiled it was him! "All right. Be that way! But I'm not leaving. Do you hear me? I'm going to stay right here and teach school whether you marry me or not."

John just kept walking away from her.

Victoria gripped her hands together in front of her— hard—and bit down on her lip. *Damn, stubborn, arrogant, know-it-all, irresistible, chauvinist swine!* If she didn't love him so much she'd be tempted to murder him.

"Do not worry," Maria said, placing a weathered hand over Victoria's clasped ones. "He is stubborn and sometimes slow to see the true way. But he will come to his senses soon. Come." She gave Victoria's hands a matter-of-fact little pat. "We must dress for the wedding."

NINA MADE A BEAUTIFUL BRIDE. Standing there under the sun and trees in the loving circle of her family and friends with her hand in that of her groom, she glowed with the special radiance of all brides everywhere. The fringe on her beautifully embroidered white tunic fell midway down her thighs, fluttering over the matching suede skirt. It was belted with a wide silver-and-turquoise concha belt, a gift from her parents. Beaded turquoise earrings dangled from her ears. Her turquoise-and-diamond engagement ring glittered on her finger.

The wedding guests stood in a circle; the bride and groom and her father, who was performing the ceremony, stood in the center. The words were in Navajo, but their meaning was clear to Victoria—love and marriage were universal concepts, calling forth universal wishes for prosperity and happiness and fertility. There was an exchange of rings, in the Anglo fashion, accompanied by the recitation of the wedding vows, and then the bride and groom fed each other a fingerful of cornmeal mush from a Navajo wedding basket with its traditional black-and-white-and-red starburst design.

Victoria looked across the circle at that moment, seeking the face of the man she loved, wishing with all her heart that it was they who were pledging their love today. She found him staring at her with an intent, furious expression on his face. She held his eyes, staring back, while Matt Redcloud delivered the concluding speech to his daughter's wedding ceremony.

She's so damned beautiful, John was thinking, not hearing a word Matt said. So damned *right*, standing there with his grandmother on one side of her and Christina on the other, looking more Navajo than many of the guests.

He'd tried not to look at her, tried desperately not to superimpose her face over that of the bride's as she said her vows, tried hopelessly not to hear his own voice repeating the same vows to her. But it was no use. All he could see was the two of them standing there—Victoria and him—pledging their love and their lives to each other. The ultimate fantasy.

It didn't help that Maria had dressed her in borrowed Indian finery again. Someone, he thought, staring at her, had done some quick work with a needle. He recognized the deep red velveteen tunic and dark green skirt with its red hemline trim as an outfit of Nina's. It fitted Victoria as if it had been made for her. The belt around her tiny waist was a woven one instead of the more usual silver and turquoise. Its fringed ends trailed down the front of her skirt, and she fingered them nervously, like worry beads, her chin up as she tried to pretend she wasn't upset.

Well, good, he thought then. *The spoiled little twit deserves to be worried and upset.* Proposing to him like that, in front of his whole family, making him a laughingstock in front of the men. She was already upsetting tradition. Already turning his life upside down. Turning his guts inside out. She *deserved* to worry. She deserved to worry a lot! And then he noticed that her arrogantly tilted chin was trembling with the effort not to cry, and he went down for the count. He knew then what he was going to do, what he'd been fated to do almost from the moment he'd laid eyes on her. But he was going to do it his way.

VICTORIA LOST SIGHT OF HIM at the conclusion of the ceremony when everyone pressed forward to offer their congratulations to the bride and groom. She pressed forward herself, trying not to make it obvious that she was looking for John, and touched her cheek to Nina's.

"Be happy," she said.

Nina's eyes twinkled at her. "You, too, my friend." She squeezed Victoria's hand. "Keep after him. He'll come around."

Victoria's eyes widened.

"Grandmother told me," Nina said, smiling. "That means she approves."

So now she had Maria Redcloud's approval, but she'd lost John's. If, she thought despondently, she had ever had it in the first place. No, she'd had it, she told herself fiercely. Had it still. He *did* love her. And if she waited long enough, he'd realize it. While she was waiting, she might as well continue to make herself useful.

"Is there anything I can do to help?" she said to Maria Redcloud, following her as she went to check on the roasting sheep.

"You can help Rose set out the food," Maria began, gesturing toward her pregnant granddaughter. "On those tables there under the trees. Rose will show—"

Her words were cut off by the sound of the pounding hooves of a horse splashing through water. Every head lifted at the noise, turning to see who was coming.

"What is it?" Maria began irritably. She stepped away from the cook fire and shaded her eyes with her hand, looking toward the rider. "Who is disturbing my granddaughter's wedding celebration with such foolishness?"

The horseman, riding bareback, was adroitly maneuvering his mount through the throng of guests.

"It's John, Grandmother," Rose said. She covered her mouth with one hand, her black eyes laughing. Her other hand rested on the swell of her belly. "And I don't think he is fooling. I think he means business."

"John? What is John—"

"You!" John said, bringing Scarlett to a halt in front of the three women. He pointed his finger at Victoria.

Her heart began to beat double time. She hadn't had to wait very long, after all. "Yes?" she said, feigning a calm she didn't feel. Suppressed laughter danced in her eyes. Joy bubbled through her blood. "Was there something you wanted?"

"You," he said again, staring down at her like a raiding warrior. His amber eyes were blazing, his jaw was set, his hard thighs gripping the back of the horse were taut under the denim of his jeans. "I want you."

"For what?" she challenged, her chin up. It wasn't trembling now. She knew "for what," but she wanted him to say it. She'd bared her soul in front of him and his family. It was time for him to bare his. "An afternoon of lust with a pampered, spoiled-rotten twit?"

"Yes, Grandson," Maria interrupted sternly, but a wide grin split her weathered apple-doll face. "What do you want with this woman?"

"I want to marry her," he said, looking at Victoria as he urged his mare next to her. "I want to give her children." He leaned down until they were almost mouth to mouth. "I want to love her," he said softly.

Victoria reached out to touch his thigh with both hands, but she could only stare back at him, speechless with delight and joy and love.

He pushed his hat back with the tip of his thumb. "Well, little lady?"

"Yes," she said, lifting her arms to wrap them around his neck as he snaked a hard forearm around her waist and hauled her onto the horse. "Oh, John, yes!"

LAUGHING BREATHLESSLY, happily, like two children chasing down the stairs on Christmas morning, they rode pell-mell through the stand of cottonwoods and peach trees that separated his hogan from those of the rest of the Redcloud clan. John dragged her off his horse, slapping the animal's backside so that it took off for the stable, and ducked through the hogan door with Victoria in his arms. She squealed as he tossed her onto the low-slung bed, giggling with anticipation and delight when he flung himself on top of her.

"Laugh at me, will you, woman?" he growled playfully, on the edge of laughter himself. And then he covered her mouth with his, and all their playfulness vanished in a blaze of searing heat and need.

His lips were hard and possessive on hers. His tongue was a loving invader—rapacious, demanding, needy as it delved into the warmth and sweetness beyond her lips. He tangled his hands in the black silk of her hair, holding her head between his palms as he told her silently, eloquently, endlessly of his love for her.

"Victoria," he breathed raggedly, when he could. His lips roamed over her face, skimming her high cheekbones, her elegant nose, her infuriating little chin. "Victoria, I'm sorry."

"Sorry?" she murmured distractedly, trying to pull his mouth back to hers. She didn't want to hear about sorry; she wanted him to go on kissing her. Forever.

"I didn't mean it when I said I didn't want you," he confessed against her open lips. "I do. I want you desperately." Their tongues touched lightly, retreated, then touched again. "I need you." He nipped at her bottom lip, tugging it gently with his teeth. "I love you."

Her arms tightened around his neck in sudden, unbearable joy. Happy tears gathered in her tightly closed eyes. "Say it again," she demanded, greedy as a child with a cookie jar within reach.

He laved her bottom lip with his tongue. "I love you."

She shivered beneath him. "Again."

His mouth hovered a mere breath above hers, waiting until she opened her eyes. "I love you, Victoria," he said then, his eyes blazing down into the melting chocolate of hers. "I don't care whether your great-grandmother was a Navajo or a Hottentot or a little green lady from Mars. I love you. And I want to marry you."

Her smile was a sight to behold, warm and teasing and full of love. "Even if I'm a pampered, spoiled-rotten twit?"

"You're no more spoiled than I am," he said solemnly, tacitly admitting the truth of what she had said to him earlier. Then he claimed her mouth again. His hand slid from her hair, down the slender column of her throat, over her chest, to cup her breast in his palm.

Victoria murmured and stirred under him, pressing herself into his hand, wishing that the velveteen fabric of her tunic would just disappear. She wanted to feel his bare hand on her bare breast. Now.

As if he sensed her need—because it echoed his own—his hand smoothed down her torso to the fringed belt at her waist and pulled at the knot that held it closed. It fell away easily, and his hand slipped under the soft fabric, over the softer skin beneath. They both sighed at the first touch of skin on skin.

"Are you wearing anything under this outfit?" John asked, his fingers feathering slowly up over her stomach toward her breast, teasing them both with the slowness of it.

"Just panties."

"Just panties?" His breathing suddenly got heavier. "No bra?"

"Just panties," she repeated, gasping as his hand covered her breast. He cupped it tenderly, gently, lovingly. "Pale pink lace with—" his thumb strummed over her nipple. She took a quick little breath. "—with little ribbon ties at the sides."

"Yeah?" Gently he rolled her nipple between his finger and thumb. "Little ribbon ties?"

"Uh-huh. All—" She licked her lips and tried again. "All you have to do is untie them."

"Yeah?" he said again. His eyes had gone from hazel to amber to gold. He abandoned her breast, reaching down to slip his hand under the hem of her full skirt. His hand was on her thigh when a shout of laughter disturbed the still, warm air of the hogan.

Victoria stopped his hand with hers. "The wedding," she said breathlessly. Until this moment, she had totally, completely forgotten about it. "They'll be wondering where we are."

John tugged his hand from under hers, moving it farther up her thigh. "No, they won't. They know where we are."

"John." She grabbed at his hand again. "It's Nina's wedding. We should probably go back."

"Don't want to." He shook her restraining hand away and yanked at the tie on her left hip.

"But someone might come looking for us."

His fingers drifted over her abdomen to her right hip. "They won't," he assured her.

"But—"

John looked down into her face, his fingers holding on to the second ribbon tie, the heel of his hand warm on her hipbone. "Do you want to go back to the party?" he asked, giving it a tiny, teasing tug. "We'll go back if you want."

Victoria hesitated, shoulds and wants warring in her.

"Last chance." He gave the ribbon another tiny tug. "Yes or no?"

"No," she said, wants winning hands down.

He pulled the knot completely loose. "Good choice." He grinned wickedly, looking for all the world like some marauding warrior leering over his helpless captive. "Because I wasn't going to let you up no matter what you said."

"No?" Victoria looked up at him from under her ebony lashes, delicious shivers of anticipation chasing their way down her spine.

"No," he said.

"Well, in that case..."

"In what case?" he prompted, tugging the untied panties away from her hips.

"Well, I've always had this fantasy..." She put her hand on the back of his neck and pulled his head down so she could whisper in his ear.

"Yeah?" He pulled back to look at her. "A sweet little lady like you has been running around with a fantasy like that in your head?"

Victoria nodded.

"Well," he said, reaching for her again, "let's get to it, then. I sure as hell haven't got anything better to do."

A scrap of pale pink lace, trailing crumpled satin ribbons, fluttered gently to the floor of the hogan.

Harlequin Temptation

COMING NEXT MONTH

ATTRACTIVE, SPACE SAVING BOOK RACK

Display your most prized novels on this handsome and sturdy book rack. The hand-rubbed walnut finish will blend into your library decor with quiet elegance, providing a practical organizer for your favorite hard-or soft-covered books.

Only $9.95

Approximately 16" x 8" when assembled

Assembles in seconds!

To order, rush your name, address and zip code, along with a check or money order for $10.70* ($9.95 plus 75¢ postage and handling) payable to *Harlequin Reader Service*:

Harlequin Reader Service
Book Rack Offer
901 Fuhrmann Blvd.
P.O. Box 1396
Buffalo, NY 14269-1396

Offer not available in Canada.

BKR-1A

*New York and Iowa residents add appropriate sales tax.

Temptation™

TEMPTATION WILL BE
EVEN HARDER TO RESIST...

In September, Temptation is presenting a sophisticated new face to the world. A fresh look that truly brings Harlequin's most intimate romances into focus.

What's more, all-time favorite authors Barbara Delinsky, Rita Clay Estrada, Jayne Ann Krentz and Vicki Lewis Thompson will join forces to help us celebrate. The result? A very special quartet of Temptations...

- **Four striking covers**
- **Four stellar authors**
- **Four sensual love stories**
- **Four variations on one spellbinding theme**

All in one great month! Give in to Temptation in September.